BLOOD IN THE SNOW

Sarah Pennington

Blood in the Snow

Front cover design by Anne Elisabeth Stengl.

Published 2018

Printed in the United States of America

ISBN: 9781726839006

This book is dedicated to my wonderful sister,
without whom the story would not exist,
and to my equally wonderful parents,
without whom I would not exist.

TABLE OF CONTENTS

CHAPTER 1

The cherry blossoms fell slowly the morning Princess Zhu Baili of the Kingdom of Seven Rivers left her home forever.

Baili tucked her hands deeper into the wide sleeves of her red silk robe, watching as the petals sprinkled the surface of the Tàiyáng River and swirled around the royal barge. She did not look at the crowds gathered on either side of the path to the barge. She did not look at the northern peaks where she would soon travel. She especially did not look at her stepmother, Empress Zhu Yawen, who stood beside her, addressing their people. She simply stared at the petals, trying and failing to focus on them instead of the empress's words.

"Though it is with great regret that I bid farewell to my stepdaughter —" the empress did not sound regretful — "her departure is undoubtedly the will of the Divine. So His prophecy commands: 'As the river unites land and sea, so the fairest of all shall unite those that have been divided and make them one.' The

Dragonglass, which cannot lie, declares Princess Baili fairer than any in the land. Therefore, she shall wed Prince Liu Xiang of the Kingdom of Three Peaks and seal between our lands a bond ushering in a new era of peace and prosperity."

She paused. The crowd did not cheer. In the ten years since the king's death, they had seen too many failed harvests and thin winters to be convinced by mere words. Even into the Palace of Crystal Springs, the rumors crept: the land was dying. The Zhu line no longer held the Divine's favor. The child heir had no Bloodgift, no right to rule. No one knew what was true and what was not, but everyone knew that an alliance with the northern empire would solve few of their problems.

Empress Yawen continued: "Because the princess's journey is dangerous and she may not return for many years, she will not depart alone. A company of our finest soldiers, led by Captain Zhihao of the Royal Guard, will see her and her attendants safely to the palace of Emperor Liu Yijun. And with her, to remind her of our hope in her, she shall bring gifts from every part of our empire, along with a special token from me."

Baili glanced in confusion at her stepmother, who drew from her sleeve a white linen handkerchief and from her sash a needle-sharp knife. "Twenty years ago, the Empress Daiyes wished for a child with hair dark as ebony, skin pale as moonlight, and lips red as the blood that bears our birthright. Saying this, she let fall three drops of her own blood into the snow. A year later, Princess Baili was born, for Empress Daiyes's gift was to have her wishes granted."

The empress paused again. Baili stared at the river and the petals, willing them to fill her mind instead of the story's end. Three drops of blood were not enough for such a great wish, and the Empress Daiyes died before she could hold her wished-for daughter. Baili knew it was not her fault, yet she wondered if she were really worth the sacrifice.

Empress Yawen ceremoniously pricked her finger and squeezed three drops of bright blood onto the handkerchief. "Now, Princess Baili, as a reminder of your heritage and a symbol of my blessing, I give you three drops of my blood which commands life. Carry them well and bring honor to those who remain here."

She held out the handkerchief. Baili turned to face her and bowed dutifully. "I . . ." she searched for words. "I thank you, honored stepmother, for your gift. I pray that I will fulfill your hopes and those of my blessed parents." Rising, she took the handkerchief and tucked it in her own sleeve.

The empress bowed slightly in return. "And now, with my blessing and the favor of the Divine, depart. May you fare well in your new home."

Baili knew this part, though the response was bitter in her mouth. "And may the Divine bless those who dwell in my once-home." She bowed thrice: to the empress, towards the crowd, and towards the Palace of Crystal Springs, her home no longer.

Then she turned away and, with measured steps, walked down the path between the rows of staring people. Her attendants fell in behind her; Dou Lanfen, her chief attendant, followed so close she nearly tread on the edge of Baili's robe. The soldiers formed ranks after them, Captain Zhihao at their head. All followed

Baili past the crowds, up the gangplank, and onto the deck of the barge.

Onboard, Baili took her place at the stern while the sailors hauled up the gangplank and cast off from the dock. She wished she could look back to see the palace, but tradition demanded she keep her gaze ahead. So, she stared towards the distant mountains while the river carried them away from all she knew and towards all that she did not.

~~~~~

For the next week and a day as they sailed up the river, Baili spent as much time on deck as possible, sketching the landscapes as they passed by. The first few days, they traveled through familiar scenes: grasslands and rice paddies and little river villages. Baili had sketched them all a hundred times before, and so she drew her charcoal pencil across the page with a confidence she felt nowhere else, taking comfort in the clean, dark lines on the white paper.

More than once, Baili wished for her ink and brushes, but Lanfen informed her that those had been packed in the hold and she knew not which box or bag they were in. So, Baili sketched and silently wished that she had temper enough to demand that Lanfen find them anyway, or, better still, that she'd left her chief attendant behind to serve someone else.

Unfortunately, she had not, and so Lanfen hovered at Baili's shoulder, apparently attentive, smiling smugly with every excuse she gave for refusing orders. Baili tried to insist, and she tried to threaten, but not until she begged, if at all, did Lanfen ever relent. After the fifth day, Baili ceased asking and started doing as much as she could for herself.

By that time, the landscapes on either side of the river had shifted. Plains became rolling hills, and thick groves of trees and bamboo appeared more and more frequently. Rice grew on terraced hillsides rather than flat ponds and pools, and other hillsides held plowed plots of still-green wheat. Even the villages perched atop hills and spilled down towards the river rather than starting at the river's edge. Baili's pen slowed as she contemplated the unfamiliar scenes, often not finishing one drawing until its source was far behind. But the added challenge only let her bury herself more deeply in her art and find in it a greater distraction from her fears and doubts.

From time to time as they journeyed, the barge captain requested that Baili use her Bloodgift to speed them on their way. Each time, she agreed gladly. With merely three drops of blood held in her hand or dropped in the river, Baili summoned breezes and currents to push the barge upstream on days when the wind stilled or blew against the sails rather than into them. As a result, they reached the foot of the mountains on the eighth day of their journey and rested that night at the city of Duānkou de Taiyáng.

At dawn the following day, they loaded bag and baggage onto the backs of oxen. Captain Zhihao helped Baili into a wicker palanquin slung between two such beasts while the soldiers and servants mounted horses and donkeys. Then they started up the winding mountain pass to Shi Xīng Jí, capital of the Kingdom of Three Peaks.

A hundred times over the mountain journey, Baili wished she were still aboard the boat. The palanquin jostled and jolted with every step of the oxen carrying it, making Baili ache all over and denying her the distraction of her sketchbook. Worse, the wicker basket trapped her. Soldiers on horseback led the oxen, and the first time Baili tried to request a halt so she could stretch her legs, Captain Zhihao informed her that they could not afford to waste time.

Baili slumped in disappointment and tried to ignore her discomfort. Before long, however, thirst overwhelmed her aches. She reached for a waterskin but found that she had none. So, she reluctantly turned to her attendants. "Lanfen, bring me my water."

Lanfen looked back at her and smiled coldly. "No, your highness."

Baili blinked and sat up straighter. *What?* Lanfen had made excuses, but never outright rebelled. Trying to ignore her misgivings, she repeated her order: "I asked you to get me water."

Lanfen, still smiling, met Baili's gaze defiantly. "You did. And I said no."

No, no, no . . . Baili took a deep breath, trying not to visibly wilt. "Will you please bring me some water?"

Lanfen ignored her. Baili licked her dry lips and looked for the other attendants, but they had ridden ahead of her palanquin to talk to the soldiers. Anyway, they had always followed Lanfen's lead aboard the ship. Next, she glanced towards the company's head. "Captain Zhihao?"

He did not respond. Baili sank back and shut her eyes. She was a princess. One day she would be an empress and unite two nations. Yet even those meant to serve and protect her refused to obey when she asked for a simple drink. How was she supposed to command a household and help rule an empire?

She tried one more time: "Captain Zhihao, call a halt. If my attendants will not serve me, then I will get my water myself."

This time the captain looked back and checked his horse so Baili and her attendants could catch up, and Baili sat up straighter, hopeful. Perhaps he had not heard her the first time. Perhaps all would be well after all. Captain Zhihao could put a stop to Lanfen's rebellion far better than Baili herself could.

But when Captain Zhihao spoke, it was not to Baili. "Dou-*shūni*, the map marks a spring near the road in only a few miles. Do you wish to stop? It will be a good place to rest if you are weary of riding.

Lanfen? He asked *Lanfen*? And, worse, addressed her as a high lady of the court, not a handmaiden? *Why have they all turned against me?* Still, Baili spoke as boldly and sternly as she could, trying to meet the captain's eyes. "Captain Zhihao, I am the princess. And I say we stop."

Captain Zhihao ignored her. "Dou-*shūni*, your orders?"

Lanfen smiled smugly. "We push on, Captain. The day is yet young, and we have many miles to go. I wish to make Shi Xīng Jí as soon as possible."

The captain nodded. "As you command." With that, he spurred his horse back to the front of the group.

Baili sank back in her basket and blinked back hot tears of despair. *I have failed already.* What kind of empress would she be if even her servants and soldiers defied the simplest requests?

No. She could not lose hope. Not now. Lanfen was eager to reach the imperial city, but once they arrived, the situation would be in Baili's favor. If only for the sake of their honor, the prince and emperor surely would not tolerate servants who defied the prince's bride-to-be. Baili could request new servants and guards and order Lanfen and Captain Zhihao and the rest back to Seven Rivers. After that, all would be well. All she had to do was endure until then.

CHAPTER 2

The day after the water incident, Captain Zhihao and his soldiers stopped reporting to Baili. Instead, they addressed warnings, comments, and requests to Lanfen, who answered as if she were the princess. As she had the first day, Baili tried to protest and, when that failed, to speak first or counter Lanfen's orders with her own. The guards ignored her save when she argued; then Captain Zhihao explained, as if to a child, why Lanfen was right and Baili was wrong. Baili gritted her teeth, listened, and tried again, but by the third day, the treatment wore her down so she only responded to the most significant exchanges.

Her attendants ignored her as well, and after several failures to make them obey, she learned to fend for herself. She slept in the open, wrapped in blankets, when her royal tent and cot proved too unwieldy to set up on her own. She fetched her own waterskin each morning and refilled it each night. She took her place in the crowd around the campfire to receive her rations from the company cook and forced herself not to complain if she received less than the others. She still rode in the palanquin, but Baili suspected that was only because Lanfen did not care to do so herself. Each day she reminded herself that if she could only endure until they reached the imperial city, all would be well.

At last, after nearly a week on the road, the captain announced, "We are within a day of Shi Xīng Jí, Dou-*shūni*."

Baili perked up. "We should push on tonight that we may arrive early tomorrow. We must not waste time now that we are so close. Is that not so, Captain?" She felt a momentary glow of pride at how regal she'd sounded. Perhaps now, so close to the city, they would remember who they were and who she was and listen at last.

"We stop here," Lanfen ordered as if Baili hadn't spoken. "We must prepare for our entrance into the city."

"You are not princess, Lanfen." Baili gripped the sides of the palanquin for support. If her company would not remember their place, she would remind them, give them one more chance. "You have forgotten yourselves, all of you. I am your princess, appointed by the Divine. Will you not give me the honor I am due?"

"You deserve no honor." Lanfen smiled as always, but even the fiercest scowl never held such malice. She held up a hand and the soldiers, including those leading the oxen, stopped. The rest of the company circled around Lanfen and Baili, spears and cudgels ready. Lanfen slid off her donkey and faced Baili. "Get down, princess."

10

You deserve no — Perhaps. Baili knew she had done nothing to earn honor, save for being born in the imperial family. But what she stood for was worth something. "I am the daughter of Emperor Zhu Aigui of the Kingdom of Seven Rivers, may he rest with the Divine in Shénme Jiāng. I bear the Divine's favor in my blood. I am destined by prophecy to unite two empires." Baili's voice shook, but she continued to speak, reminding herself as well as her company. "If you will not honor me, then honor my family, my heritage, my destiny. In not doing so, you bring dishonor on yourselves and your families for this — this *treason*."

"It is not treason if the empress, may she reign a thousand years, orders it." Lanfen beckoned to the soldiers holding the oxen. "If she will not come, bring her to me."

The soldiers dismounted. Baili reached for her knife but found only soft folds of silk. *What* — She pulled away as the soldiers reached for her. "You cannot —"

They grasped her by the shoulders and lifted her from the basket. Baili kicked and pulled, but they held her tight and carried her to Lanfen as easily as they would a child. They dropped Baili at Lanfen's feet so she fell to her knees, and then they stepped back, hands on cudgels, ready to strike.

Lanfen scornfully stared down at Baili. "Now you see how it is. You were always meant to kneel."

"No — I am your *princess* —" Baili started to stand, but a soldier kicked her back down immediately.

"By the empress's command, you are *nobody's* princess." Lanfen lost her smile and drew a knife, long and deadlier than Baili's. "Empress Yawen ordered that you not reach the city, that one better suited to your role take your place."

"You mean yourself." Baili pressed her knuckles into the dirt, fixed her gaze on the knife in Lanfen's hand. No wonder her soldiers and attendants ignored her! Why should they serve when they intended to betray her later?

"Naturally. Few in Three Peaks have seen Princess Baili in over a year; most have never seen her. When I arrive, dressed in royal robes and bearing the imperial seal, they shall have no reason to doubt." Lanfen gestured with the knife. "Now, remove your robe and give it to me."

"No." Baili's mind raced. *She's going to* kill *me. Kill me and take my name. I won't let her. I can overpower her if I can get her knife . . .*

"You do not have the right to refuse orders any longer." Lanfen's hand twitched. "Remove your robe or it will be removed for you."

"N — Not *here*." Baili refused to think about Lanfen's threats. She instead focused on a memory, of instructions from an old soldier who taught the emperor's daughters how to act if kidnapped. "*Let them think themselves in control,"* he had said. *"Let them become arrogant. Then they will not expect your move."*

Lanfen was arrogant already. Making her more so would not be difficult. "Please, Dou-*shūni*. Please, even if you take everything else, leave me the small dignity of not being exposed before men. Take me aside and do what you must, but please grant me this."

"We should not risk it, Dou-*shūni*," Captain Zhihao said. "What if she escapes?"

"She will not escape." Lanfen shook her head dismissively. "You do not know the princess, Captain. She is too timid to act and too weak to fight so long as she does not bleed. My attendants and I will see to this. We are not so without honor that we cannot afford small mercies." She sheathed her knife and motioned to Baili. "Stand up. Jiang, Lei, hold her so she cannot run."

Baili stood, keeping her head bowed, and the two attendants grasped her arms. Lanfen led them off the path, five yards into the trees, and stopped beneath a gnarled fir tree. "There. Your dignity is safe. Now, your robe."

Baili fumbled with her sash, slowly working the knot free. She needed to buy time; she needed answers . . . "Please, Dou-*shūni*, why this?"

"Because the empress orders it." Lanfen watched her, hawklike. "When you are gone, she will again be fairest and bear the prophecy. And she will fulfill it better, not with a mere treaty but by adding the lands of Three Peaks to our own Seven Rivers."

"You speak of conquest." The knot came loose, and Baili unwound the pale silk. "She would not dare — so soon after the treaty — That is great dishonor, to give and break your word in one breath."

"This is why you must be replaced," Lanfen scoffed. "You do not understand: great dishonor may bring glory and greater honor later. And how great the honor of the one sitting on the throne of the world and of those who faithfully serve her?" A fierce smile flashed across her face before she grew cold again. "Enough talk. Your robe."

"Yes, Dou-*shūni*." Baili pulled away the last loop of her sash and let her robe slip from her shoulders, revealing her white shift. Then, glancing upward, she hurled her robe over Lanfen's head, threw her sash in the face of an attendant, and bolted.

The remaining attendant lunged and grabbed her wrist. Baili kicked backward, but lost her balance and fell in the dirt. She strained against the woman's grasp, trying to regain her feet, gaze fixed on the thorny vine wrapped around a nearby tree.

The other attendant grasped Baili's other arm. The two jerked her to her feet and turned her to face Lanfen, who stood with the robe crumpled in her arms, her bun skewed and her expression twisted in anger. "Very clever." She pointed towards a tree that appeared vine-free. "Bind her. She must be dead the moment her blood flows."

"As you wish, Dou-*shūni*." The attendants dragged Baili towards the tree, forced her to kneel among the roots, and pulled her arms back to wrap around the trunk. Then they bound her wrists and shoulders, and one held her head in place as Lanfen again drew her knife.

Divine, save me. Baili kept her eyes on Lanfen's knife as she scraped her wrists against the rough bark and probed the tree with her fingers. "Please — please — do not do this —" Her fingertips found the end of a thin vine covered in razor-sharp thorns. As Lanfen stepped toward her, Baili squeezed the plant between her fingers. The thorns stung as they pierced her skin, and Baili felt sticky blood on her hand.

This was why the Divine had given Bloodgifts, the stories said. So that when His chosen rulers were in utmost danger, when they lost all other hope, when they sat bound and usurpers smiled in triumph, they would have one last defense. Three drops of blood in the sky or river could summon breeze or current enough to propel a ship; three drops in the snow could wish a child into existence.

Baili held far more than three drops now.

CHAPTER 3

Lanfen leaned down and set her knife against Baili's throat. "Your reign is over, princess. Hope that the Divine grants you a place among your ancestors though you yourself will never become one."

Baili didn't respond. She shut her eyes, focused, and summoned a wind far stiffer and stronger than any she'd called before. It rushed around the tree and slammed into Lanfen, who stumbled backward. The attendants released Baili and drew their own knives, but Baili turned the wind on them, knocking them back as well.

Baili's palm tingled. She didn't know if that meant she needed more blood or simply that she had, after all, grabbed a thorn vine and given herself many cuts that would probably become infected later. Just in case, she flexed her fingers, forcing more blood to the surface. Then she drew the breezes into a cyclone around herself and her tree. As the winds spun, they caught stones and branches from the ground, forming a barrier between Baili and her traitorous attendants.

Safe for the moment, she wriggled and twisted her hands, trying to loosen the knotted cords. After a few seconds, she gave up and attempted instead to catch her bonds against the thorns. *If only I had Lanfen's knife!* But too late for that.

Outside the barrier, Lanfen shouted: "Captain Zhihao! Bring your men and come quickly!"

Baili bit her lip. Somehow, she had to escape before the soldiers arrived. They couldn't cross her wall of wind, true, but they could kill her far more easily than Lanfen could once she finally had to release the cyclone and run.

Let's try this. Baili squeezed the vine again with each hand, ignoring the resulting sharp streaks of pain. Then she pushed the winds outwards in a circle, throwing Lanfen and the two attendants to the ground and pelting them with debris. Then, as soldiers crashed through the foliage, Baili drew air within first one knot and then the other, forcing the cords apart. She jerked her hands free and stumbled to her feet.

"No!" Lanfen, standing again, lunged towards Baili.

Baili turned and threw up her hands. A new breeze flung Lanfen back. Then Baili darted around the tree and ran like she had never run before. She heard Lanfen's voice behind her; heard the soldiers pushing through the branches. Her palms stung as if she'd dipped her wounded hands in lemon juice. She flexed her fingers, but movement just shot new pain through the injuries.

Where am I going? Soon she would grow tired and the soldiers would catch her and kill her. Already her legs began to ache and her side and lungs to burn.

17

Perhaps she could hold the soldiers off for a little while with her Bloodgift if they didn't shoot her first, but she wouldn't last forever.

Baili dodged around a tree, glanced back. She couldn't quite see the soldiers, but she could hear them. Their shouts and footsteps drew closer every minute.

Then, ahead of her, she heard another sound: rushing water. *Oh, thank the Divine.* Baili angled to the left, towards the sound. Thorns and branches caught at her shift as she ran, and she gave thanks that Lanfen had taken her bulky robe. Stones cut through her silken slippers, slicing into her feet like knives. Good. More blood, more power. Never mind the pain, never mind that every step hurt like walking on shattered glass. It was better than dying.

Up ahead, the trees thinned out and the ground dropped away into a cliff. Baili glanced back again. Now she could see the soldiers gaining on her with each step. *Please, Divine . . .*

She passed a thorn tree and squeezed one of its branches. No matter what happened next, she needed all the blood and power she had. *Ten yards more.* Yet the soldiers were nearly on her, and her legs were faltering . . .

A hand grabbed the back of her shift and yanked. Baili yelped and stumbled back, twisting as she fell. She flailed wildly at the soldier, buffeting him with air until a lucky blow forced him to let go. Baili dropped to the ground, rolled, and scrambled up as other soldiers closed in. Before they could catch her, she sprinted the last few yards to the cliff. At its edge, she hesitated a split second, but a glance back at the soldiers still charging towards her made up her mind. Without giving herself any more time to think, she leapt and fell towards the water below.

Baili barely had time to think as she dropped. One moment, she felt like she soared; the next, she saw the white-tipped river surface hurtling towards her at a ferocious speed. She hit with a stinging smack and sank into its dark depths. Blackness sparkled in her vision, and she gasped for breath but found only water. *No! No!* She clawed at the river, trying to fight her way to the surface even as her momentum carried her deeper. *I will* not *die in something I can control!*

A force from below pushed her upwards. Her head broke the surface, and she gulped for air, then coughed violently as she expelled the water from her lungs. The current carried her towards a large rock, and she caught hold of it and clung there, coughing and gasping until she could breathe normally.

Only then did Baili look upwards. She saw no soldiers, no archers, no one climbing down the steep sides or waiting at the top. Perhaps they assumed that the force of the fall had killed her, or that she'd drowned in the river.

Baili shuddered and tightened her grip on the rock. *I . . . I should not be alive. How am I alive?* She stared at the cliff, taking in deep, shuddering breaths. *I . . . I just jumped off . . . off of . . . off that. Oh my. I jumped. Off that. Oh Divine . . .*

She shivered as a breeze blew across the river's surface and right through her sodden shift. Her wet hair, loose from its bun, clung to her face and shoulders. *The empress ordered . . . and Lanfen . . .*

19

*and Captain Zhihao . . . they tried to . . . and I jumped
. . .*

Baili shut her eyes and rested her head against the rock. *I am* never *doing this again.* Once she reached safety, she would never leave. She'd sit in her room and walk in the garden and paint and nothing more. *But I suppose I have to find safety first.*

Where was safe? Not home. If Lanfen spoke the truth, if Empress Yawen wanted her dead and planned to attack the Kingdom of Three Peaks, Baili would be assassinated within a month. She would die of poison in her tea or a dart in her neck rather than a knife at her throat, but death was death. And even if the Palace of Crystal Springs were safe, she would have to find her way back alone, with no food or guidance.

On the other hand, Shi Xīng Jí lay within a day's travel, on the river's path. With her gift, Baili could float through the night and reach the city in the early morning. From there, she could go to Lord Chion, the Seven Rivers diplomat — No, he would be on Yawen's side. A Three Peaks noble, then. Perhaps even the emperor himself. Even in her state, her Bloodgift would be proof enough to gain her an audience with *someone.*

To Shi Xīng Jí, then. Baili released the rock and grabbed a length of fallen tree floating by. Supporting herself on it, she willed the water around her to flow backward. Her personal current quickly gained strength and carried her away towards the city.

~~~~~

Baili reached the city in the grey predawn, nearly fainting from weariness. She'd dared not rest on the river for fear that her power would run out while she slept or that someone would spot her while she lay senseless. Other worries kept her awake as well. What would happen if Seven Rivers and Three Peaks went to war? The question made Baili shudder. The two empires had not fought in years, aside from quickly settled skirmishes in outer provinces. Both sides implicitly acknowledged that they were too evenly matched; war would cripple both nations. Then they would be vulnerable to revolt in their provinces and invasion by the Plains clans. Surely Yawen had thought of all this and made a plan to prevent it, but what it was Baili couldn't guess.

The sight of the city temporarily drove away thoughts of both weariness and war. It sprawled in the valley between the three greatest peaks in the range, on the bend formed by the Taìyáng and a second river, the Yueláng. Older than Shi Chunshi, Baili's home, it had many times grown beyond its walls and watchtowers and now encroached on both riverbanks. Baili studied it with bleary eyes as she directed her log off the Taìyáng and up the second river towards the castle, which stood on Mount Rìchū's slopes.

The river carried Baili past the palace and city to slopes of rock and grass that looked like pastureland. There, Baili directed her log to the bank and climbed onto dry ground. What now? She needed to find proper clothes before she went to the palace, but no one would be awake until sunrise. And she could barely keep her eyes open . . . Surely an hour of sleep would do no harm?

With that thought in mind, she stumbled up the slope towards a willow tree whose branches formed a thick, leafy curtain hanging to the ground. *I'll be safe there*. Even if someone came before she woke, they would never see her. She could rest until dawn. Satisfied, she curled up among the roots and fell into the deep sleep of exhaustion.

CHAPTER 4

Baili realized something was wrong the moment she awoke. Had she not gone to sleep under a tree? Yet the ground beneath her was smooth, and her cheek rested on fabric. She had emerged from the river wearing only her sodden shift, but now a rough robe smelling of horse wrapped around her. Rather than being cold and damp, a fire's warmth crackled at her back. Rain fell on a roof, but none touched her. And she heard unfamiliar voices, strangely accented, speaking in a mix of her own tongue and a language — no, two languages — she did not know.

Had she been found, then? By whom? Baili half-opened her eyes and peered between her lashes. She seemed to be in a small, dim hut. Directly before her stood a low table, at which two young men and a woman the same age sat. Another man, slightly older, sat against the far wall, half-hidden by shadows.

The two speakers did not sit but rather stood on opposite sides of the table. One was a woman Baili's age, but taller, slimmer, and darker. Six twisted braids wrapped into a loose bun atop her head, and her narrow face was set in an expression harder than mountain stone. Shoulders back, arms crossed over her sturdy brown robe, she defiantly faced her opponent, a man not much taller but several years older than she. He wore no robe but rather a sleeveless shirt and loose pants tucked into well-worn boots. Thick brows drew together over his heavy-featured face, and he scowled in clear frustration at the woman. Oddly for a man, he wore his stringy hair down to his shoulders, half in thick braids and half loose.

The man, who had been ranting in his own language, switched to Baili's tongue. "I have spoken once; so I will speak again: we cannot turn her out! Such is not to your honor or mine. She comes to us in need and with us she remains until she wishes to go."

"Why should she? What have we to do with her?" the woman shot back. "She is a foolish *yofukashi* who has lost her wits and way. Nothing more! And you are a foolish man to think she is worth helping!"

"She is no camp-follower. Look at her, blind woman!" The man gestured at Baili. "A traveler, lost and hurt! Perhaps an angel of the endless skies, come from the Five Above to test us! I saw her ride the river against its current before she lay beneath the willow, shivering and wounded. No camp-follower would do this! Even if she were — deny that she needs help, blind one! Deny if you can!"

"Do not call *me* blind, Ganbaatar! We shall decide fairly." The woman addressed the three seated at the table. "Who else sees what this fool cannot, that the girl is a *yofukashi* who has brought her trouble on herself?"

24

One of the men at the table lifted a hand and, after a moment, the woman seated beside him did as well. The arguing woman huffed. "Of course you agree with the fool, Nianzu. Azuma?" She glanced towards the man by the wall. "What say you? Come, tell the horse-fool that he is blind."

Azuma looked directly at Baili. "I will not call either you or Gan sightless, Chouko. I am not the one to ask. The girl has woken; let her tell her story."

"Has she?" The woman — Chouko — turned on Baili. "Are you awake, girl?"

Baili reluctantly opened her eyes all the way and sat up. "I am, honored hostess. I beg your forgiveness for whatever trouble I have caused." She bent at the waist until her nose nearly touched her knees as if meeting a royal of her own rank. A voice in the back of her head said she shouldn't bow so to a peasant, but not being thrown out on her ear seemed more important than dignity.

Chouko's expression did not soften, but her eyebrows rose slightly. Ganbaatar smirked. "See, *erveekei*? No camp-follower has such manners. She is an angel of the skies, as I said." Arm across his chest, he half-bowed. "You are welcome in my tents, pretty angel. I am Ganbaatar, Rider of the *Salkhi* Clan. The angry woman is Nakuhara Chouko of the Isles of Rising Fire. Do not be troubled by her; she is only happy when she has something to frown at. My sole defender is Jīn Nianzu, and the others with him are Li Renshu and his sister, Jialin. The one who sits alone is Haraku Azuma, also of the Isles. Now, pretty angel, who are you?"

"I am honored to meet all of you." Baili bowed again, less deeply. "I am called Baili, of the Kingdom of Seven Rivers. May I ask how I came here? I remember nothing since I lay beneath the willow, too weary to continue my journey."

"*Gan* is how you came here." Chouko huffed. "He saw your arrival and abandoned his duties to bring you here this morning, thinking that you needed aid and that it was his duty to provide it, however little he has to offer. But I wish to know where you journeyed from and why, Baili-of-Seven-Rivers."

"I . . ." Baili paused. She dared not reveal her true identity, but she needed an explanation that would let her go to the palace later. "I am a maidservant to the princess of Seven Rivers, but I became separated from our company. I made my way here on my own, hoping to find them again at the palace. Has the princess yet arrived?"

"She has. Gan and I tended to her company's horses this afternoon," replied Nianzu. "Now she sits at feast with the emperor and his court."

"Then I will seek her." Baili stood, though her legs shook. "I do not wish to cause you trouble. If you might tell me where to find proper clothes, I will go." If all went well, she could expose Lanfen before the whole court, though the emperor might not be pleased at being interrupted during his banquet. At the thought of food, her stomach growled, and she blushed in embarrassment.

"You cannot go," Jialin said. "You have no money, and the shops and charities are closed."

"Nor will you find shelter if the palace guards turn you away," Azuma added. "For good or ill, you have

26

come to us. Better that you stay with us tonight and go to the palace in the morning. We have little, but we can offer this much, can we not, Chouko?"

"Of course, since she is here." Chouko huffed, scowling more deeply. "What Gan has started, we must finish." She addressed Baili once more. "Be welcome in our home. You may eat, stay the night, and save us all from Gan's sulking over his honor."

Baili hesitated. Never had a welcome felt so unwelcoming, and surely these people had little to share. But to refuse would be rude, and Jialin and Azuma had a point. So she bowed again as she replied, "I thank you for your welcome, gracious hostess. May your blessings upon me return to you."

"We accept your thanks. Be seated at our table." Chouko stepped past Baili to collect two stacks of rough clay bowls from the mantel. "Ailin will arrive soon; then we will eat."

Baili sat down facing Gan and the door. Azuma silently joined the group at the table as well. Chouko did not sit but busied herself setting a large bowl and a pair of chopsticks before each person and filling smaller bowls with water from a cask in the corner. She had nearly finished when the door swung open and a woman about Azuma's age, old enough that Baili wondered that she wasn't a mother already, entered.

The woman was surprisingly round for her station, with a face broader and darker than Lanfen's, and she carried a woven basket on each arm. "Chouko! See what I have! They had a whole pot of dumplings they could not serve, so Huan gave me half — *oh*!" Her gaze fell on Baili and widened in recognition and

27

surprise. "What — how — *your highness*!" And before Baili could say or do anything to stop her, Ailin dropped to her knees and bowed.

CHAPTER 5

"What?" several voices demanded at once. Chouko scoffed and set down the last bowl. "Do not speak nonsense, Ailin. The princess would not sit in our hut when she can feast in the emperor's hall. This is a lost traveler Gan dragged in, nothing more. Get up and join us."

Ailin didn't move. "Surely you know what you know, Chouko, but I know what I have seen. I lived for eighteen years in the Shi Chunshi and served in the royal palace for five. I have seen Princess Baili, and I have seen a woman who claims to be her, and now I see the true princess sitting at our table."

Chouko shook her head. "You lived there three years ago. Surely the princess has changed since then."

"Chouko, she may speak truth." Nianzu leaned forward and dropped his voice. "Gan and I have heard similar whispers. Many workers from the lower kingdom say the princess in the palace looks different than the princess they remember, and some have only been here a few months."

"And what does time matter? One does not forget the face of the fairest in the land and the fulfillment of wish and prophecy," Ailin insisted. "I tell you, this is she!"

"Enough," Gan interrupted. "Let our guest tell us." He turned and faced Baili. "Are you who Ailin says, pretty angel?"

Oh, Divine, please no. Why, out of all the huts and homes in Shi Xīng Jí, had she been brought to the one where someone would recognize her on sight? *Then again, if others recognize that Lanfen isn't me . . .* The thought lightened her heart the slightest bit. Whatever happened, at least someone would know a tiny piece of the truth, even if they were only servants and animal keepers.

That didn't solve her situation now, though. What should she say? She could hold to the story she'd given earlier, but she had no guarantee that they would believe her over Ailin, nor that Ailin herself would be convinced. On the other hand, if she confirmed Ailin's words . . . Perhaps they would turn her over to Lanfen, hoping for a reward from the one currently in power, but Ailin, at least, seemed to still be loyal to Baili.

She had no choice; she had to risk it. "I am." Baili forced herself to hold her head high, to speak as the princess she was, though her voice trembled and she wished she could curl into herself and escape the stares of those around her. "I am Zhu Baili, princess of the Kingdom of Seven Rivers, eldest daughter of Emperor Zhu Aigui, may he rest in honor with his ancestors, and betrothed of Prince Liu Xiang of the Kingdom of Three Peaks. As I traveled to your land, my company sought to kill me and replace me with the woman who now sits in my place. By the grace of the Divine and the gift which He bestowed on my blood, I escaped, and the river carried me here. I beg your forgiveness for hiding my identity, but I did not know by whom I had been found." She took a deep breath and focused on Ailin. "Rise . . ." she hesitated, realizing she didn't know the woman's family name. "Um. Rise, Ailin. I thank you for the honor you show me."

Ailin stood, keeping her gaze averted. "I seek to serve you however I may, your highness."

Gan laughed — *laughed*! "And Chouko claims I carried in a camp-follower! Be doubly welcome in my tents, *günja*. What is mine, may it be yours."

The others murmured polite words of welcome as well, except Chouko, who put her hands on her hips and stared Baili in the face as defiantly as Lanfen ever had. "You are welcome here, princess — but what now? I suppose you wish us to bow and serve as if you sat with the emperor after all? No doubt you desire us to find you a feast since we now know your title?"

"I . . ." Baili balled her hands in her sleeves. Should she push back? Insist on proper respect, though not the special treatment Chouko implied? But what if she did? She dared not alienate her hosts, and if worst came to worst, the others would surely back Chouko. And in any case, she didn't *want* to push back. She wanted to drink something hot and eat dinner and have a good night's sleep before she faced

Lanfen in the morning. That would be confrontation enough.

So, Baili shook her head and pushed a smile. "I ask for nothing more than what you offered before. Let me be a humble lost traveler at your table; let me have a bite of food and a mat on which to sleep, and when morning comes I will trouble you no more. Will you do this for me, gracious hostess?"

Chouko's eyebrows rose, but she dipped in a half-bow. "Very well. As you ask, so you will have." She turned. "Ailin, the dumplings. We have all waited long enough for dinner."

~~~~~

The next morning, Jialin woke Baili with a shake to the shoulder and a proffered peach. "Breakfast," she explained, as Baili sleepily took the fruit. Then, sliding a folded length of green cloth from her arm, she added, "And a fresh robe, brought by Gan, highness."

"Gan? How?" Baili accepted the robe and shook it out. It was not silk but linen like the palace servants wore. The color was variegated as if the dying process had gone wrong. "Where did he get it?"

Jialin shrugged. "I don't know, highness. Gan is Gan. He does things, and we do not ask questions. Not anymore. We think, though, that he must have either many friends or many enemies."

"But . . . but he's . . ." Baili trailed off, not wanting to say "He's just a servant." After all, so was Jialin. "Why?"

"He is Gan," Jialin repeated, folding her hands. "And he feels that you are his responsibility as his guest. It is the way of his people." With that, she bowed and hurried to the door.

Baili stared, processing the conversation. Then she slipped off the rough robe she'd been wearing and put on the green one. She had lost the sticks and pins that held up her bun, but she combed her hair as best she could with her fingers and tucked it back behind her shoulders. Then she walked to the door, carrying her peach and the brown robe.

Outside, she found Gan, Chouko, and Nianzu waiting. She bowed to Gan. "I thank you for your gift, sir."

"Of course, *günja*. You cannot go to the palace wearing my robe." Gan took the brown robe and wrapped it around himself. On him, it came only down to his knees. "We will escort you there if you are ready. We two —" he indicated himself and Nianzu — "must go that way to the emperor's stables, and I would see you safely on your way."

Baili glanced at Chouko. "What of you? You are coming as well?"

Chouko folded her arms. "I am. It is not far from my path, and someone must keep these two from playing the fool and the hero at once."

"Thank you?" Baili hesitated. "Shall we go, then?"

"You do not need to thank us, except perhaps Chouko. It may shock her out of scowling for five minutes. And yes, we go." Gan set off up the dirt path leading past the huts, up a hill, towards the palace, and the others followed.

The road took them past various other cottages and outbuildings, which Baili guessed housed other outdoor laborers. Beyond those lay the pens and barns for the livestock and, farther still, fields and orchards. Gan led them away from these and around the ornamented wall that surrounded the courtyard and palace proper, towards the public gate.

As they walked, Baili mentally rehearsed what to say and do. She'd use her Bloodgift to get their attention. If only she had a knife! She flexed her hands; they hurt, as did her feet, but they were already healing, with no sign of infection. Perhaps she could find more thorns somewhere. What words could she use? *"Worthy soldiers, my name is Zhu Baili —"* and then she'd need her full list of titles, wouldn't she? After that . . . *"The woman whom your emperor received yesterday was no true princess, but rather my servant, who turned against me on the road two days ago. I ask to see your commander, that he might aid me in removing this rebel."*

Should she mention her stepmother's plans for conquest? No. Not to the common soldiers, as long as they let her in. Better not to alarm them yet. Even with her Bloodgift, she would have enough trouble convincing the guards to believe that she was who she claimed she was.

Gan stopped a short distance from the gate and guardpost. "Listen, they are changing the guard. We will wait and perhaps hear something worth knowing."

Baili nodded and held her breath, listening as the soldiers spoke.

"Lin Du reporting for guard duty." This was a young voice; Baili imagined he would be about her own age, perhaps just in his first year of service.

"Took you long enough." This voice sounded older, like that of a man who'd served several years and been on at least one campaign — though perhaps that was just the effect of weariness. "Guard relinquished, and gladly. Watch well."

"So I shall. Anything to report?"

"Nothing — Ah, one thing. A new order from the emperor." The soldier yawned. "It seems that the river-princess traveled here with her royal cousin, but this cousin tried to murder her on the road so she could take her place."

"And the traitor escaped?"

"So the princess claims, and now she fears that her cousin will come and try to say that she is the true princess. She and the princess bear the same Bloodgift, control of wind and water, so she may attempt to use that as proof of her claims. The emperor commands that if this woman appears, we pretend to listen to and obey whatever she says, then escort her to the dungeons."

Baili sank against the wall in defeat. *I should have known . . .* Why had she thought she could simply walk in and announce herself? Lanfen was no fool; she would guess that a water-controlling princess could survive a river. And she knew how Baili would prove her identity — undoubtedly she had used some of those words and signs herself — and had ensured that the surest proof, her Bloodgift, would become marks of a traitor. Had Baili arrived at the gates only ten minutes later, she would have walked straight into a trap.

But now what? She could not announce herself as she planned. If the emperor were in possession of a

Dragonglass, she could appeal to that, but she knew he was not. She could not go home; she could not go to the emperor; what was left?

Gan muttered something under his breath and turned back the way they'd come. Chouko huffed and followed him with Nianzu. Baili trailed after, hanging back more than before. What if they too believed Lanfen's message? None of them would be pleased to think themselves tricked, not after they'd helped her.

The three stopped on the far side of the palace, and Gan faced Baili. "She has you well penned, *günja*. I do not think you will take what is yours today."

"No. I do not think so either." Baili glanced from one face to another. "You do not believe the guard?"

"Of course not." Nianzu shook his head. "We trust Ailin and the others from your land. And if you were who they claim, you would have declared yourself princess immediately and demanded honor. Besides, no one serving in the castle, so far as we have heard, knew anything of a cousin journeying with the princess."

"Thank you." Baili managed a slight smile. "I suppose I ought to seek a place to stay in the city until I decide what to do next. Perhaps I can find work; do you know where I might look?"

Chouko raised an eyebrow. "*You'll* find little honest work. Most want skilled workers, not pampered dolls. Alone, you would be safer to walk up to the guards and tell them who you are."

"Then what do you say I do?" Baili balled her fists. "I am not as wise and worldly as you, honored hostess, but even I know that one must work in order to eat. I will learn what I must to survive."

"You fret too much, *günja*." Gan flashed a smile. "You will remain with us, unless you wish otherwise. You are still our guest, and so we will take care of you."

Baili shook her head. "You need not. You have done so much already, and I would only burden you."

Chouko snorted again. "You waste time protesting. Gan says you will stay, and so you will stay and save us his sulking. You will not impose; you said you wish to work, and I am due a helper in keeping the geese. *They* do not care if you are experienced or not. Or are you too fine to chase birds?"

"I . . ." Baili hesitated. Keeping geese sounded easy enough, but doing that with Chouko was another thing entirely. *What choice do I have?* Chouko was right; she wouldn't find much other work. This would keep her near the palace but out of Lanfen's view. And perhaps Gan and the others could help her come up with a new plan. She could survive Chouko until then. So, Baili bowed and said, "You honor me with your offer of aid. I accept gladly, with most humble thanks."

Chouko's mouth and eyebrows twitched. "Very well, then." She waved a hand at Gan and Nianzu. "Go to your work before you are late. You —" she turned back to Baili — "will come with me. We must tell the overseer that Ailin's cousin has come looking for work and that I wish for her help. And then we shall see how well a princess can tend geese."

CHAPTER 6

Baili soon reached a very firm conclusion: the reason Chouko tended the emperor's geese was that her temperament matched theirs exactly. Tigers in stories might lay their heads in princesses' laps; bears would bring them honey and fruit rather than devour them; snakes would never dare to strike any except their foes. But geese bowed the neck to no one, princesses least of all. They hissed when she came near and snapped at her skirts when she tried to herd them up the path after Chouko. A few actually bit her before they reached the river, and others buffeted and bruised her legs with wings and beaks. Only quick use of the bamboo staff she'd been given kept her from being seriously injured.

Once the geese were finally paddling in the river shallows and grazing along the banks, Baili turned to Chouko. "I do not think you needed help, honored hostess. The geese obey *you*."

"You only have to show that you do not fear them and will push back if they peck." As if on cue, one of the geese ran into Baili's skirts while chasing a bug and hissed. Chouko hissed back and shoved it away with her staff. "And no one would look for a *kuīnzuko* among the geese."

"That is true." Baili forced a laugh. "And even if I am found, perhaps the geese will attack my enemies and I will be safe."

"So they might, and so you would." Chouko smiled proudly. "They are fierce as tigers and give up less easily."

"I am sure." Baili sighed and sat down in the grass atop the bank. "What did you call me a moment ago? *Kuīn . . .*?"

"*Kuīnzuko.* It is your title in my language, same as *günja* in Gan's." Chouko's tone took on a bitter note. "You *jaken-sha*. You conquer half the world, trade with the rest, yet learn no one's language but your own."

"My apologies?" Baili fidgeted with the too-short sleeves of her robe. "You are from the Isles of Rising Fire, yes? How did you come here?"

"You cannot guess? Your kingdoms have been trying to conquer the *Kasai Shotō* for years." Chouko stared past the geese, towards the east. "My home and many other islands, they did conquer, and they brought many here to work. That was before your emperor died and many river-peoples came north because their own land was dying."

People are leaving Seven Rivers? Baili knew times were hard in her home, but she hadn't realized how hard. "Is that why Ailin came here?"

"No." Chouko shook her head. "She was married young, to a man of dark temper. Then he murdered another man, and when she heard, she fled here in fear. She took one job and another and another, honest and not, before Gan found her and got her a place with us."

"Oh." Baili ran her fingers through the grass. None of this was her fault, yet Chouko's tone made her feel like every ounce of the blame lay on her shoulders. "And Gan? We have not conquered the Endless Plains, and their land thrives. Why is he here?"

"Captured in battle, I think." Chouko shrugged, relaxing. "It is hard to tell; he says little about himself. But he must have been a warrior; he slaved two years in the west of the empire, rebuilding the walls of Shi Tienkon, just as Azuma did, before the emperor's men brought him here to tend and train the horses."

"Ah. That is like my home." Baili recalled what she had heard from other nobles. "Plainsmen handle the horses like no others, and they can tame even the wildest stallions. And they love horses so greatly that they will not hurt even an enemy's steeds."

"I think *that* is more honor than horse-love. Gan would call hurting your foe through his horse a coward's trick." Chouko snorted. "Fool man." Her tone became quieter. "I wish I knew why you and yours must bring those like my family here. Surely your people can tend your own geese and goats, if not your horses. If you must conquer us, conquer us, but let us remain in our own homes!"

"We . . . Yes, we could." Baili hesitated, searching for the right words. "It is a mark of status, of power, in the Inner Kingdoms to have many foreign servants working your lands and more so to have them serving within your very home, especially at your table."

"I see." Chouko's tone was not accusatory so much as utterly flat. "Tell me, *kuīnzuko*, did captives of your empire's conquests wait on your table?"

"Yes." Baili stared at the bamboo staff resting across her knees, not daring to look Chouko's way. "But I did not consider until now what that meant for them."

"Of course not. *Kuīnzuko.*" Chouko spat the word like a curse, stood, and stalked away.

Baili stayed sitting, watching the breeze in the grass and the geese in the river and searching for refuge in mentally painting the scene. But try as she might, she couldn't focus on strokes of light and color when hard truth stared her in the face. The horrors of conquest and war were supposed to be over. Few countries resisted now if Seven Rivers or Three Peaks sought to add to their empires, and if they didn't resist, the conquering empire took no captives. The country's rulers still reigned as long as they swore fealty to the emperor, and in return for a portion of crops and coin each year, the country received protection from the other empire and increased trade with the conqueror's other holdings. The arrangement was supposed to be good for both sides, yet Chouko's situation told a different story.

Putting captured soldiers to work was one thing. That gave them a chance to repay the damage they'd done rather than languishing in some dungeon. But tearing families from their homes to increase your own status . . .

It's not right. How did she not see that before? Baili knew the answer without thinking about it. She'd barely noticed the servants in the Palace of Crystal Springs, barely considered that they had lives outside their service to her family. She'd been too caught up in her artwork, in her fears for the future, in trying to pretend to the court that she was worthy of the destiny before her. Now she knew better. But what could she do? Even as princess and fulfillment of prophecy, she'd had little power to change anything. Now she had even less.

An empress has power. The emperor's first wife not only guided her household but also advised her husband. If she could find the courage and the words, if she could make Prince Xiang understand what she now knew, perhaps she could make a change. Perhaps she could set things right and, in doing so, accomplish something to make her mother's sacrifice truly worthwhile.

But if she wanted to do any of that, she'd have to become empress. And becoming empress meant exposing Lanfen, reclaiming her place, and marrying the prince. Baili glanced back towards the palace with a sigh. She needed a plan, but with the emperor apparently on Lanfen's side, she had no idea where to begin. *Oh, Divine, please, help me think of something, and soon!*

CHAPTER 7

Baili did not think of a plan that day, nor any day the next week. Her newfound companions among the animal keepers slowly accepted her, seeming to assume that a princess with no standing wasn't really much higher in rank than they were. Jialin, despite her initial shyness, warmed up to Baili soonest, begging stories of life in the Kingdom of Seven Rivers, which Baili shared gladly. In return, at Baili's request, Jialin told of her and Renshu's former life growing up in a small mountain village, of early years spent roaming the forests together during every spare moment and of their decision to leave and seek a better life in the city after their parents' deaths. Renshu quickly joined in, correcting Jialin on various details and adding his own perspective on the events she recounted.

Nianzu, too, eventually shared his own story at Baili's prompting, speaking of his life in Duānkou de Yuèláng, a city in the north of the Kingdom of Three Peaks, of his parents, both weavers, and his two elder brothers. "They are why I am here," he added, smiling wryly. "All three of us cannot inherit the business when my father dies, and even if we could, I do not want to be trapped in a weaver's shop all my life. But after I failed two apprenticeships at home, no one else there would take me on, so I came here, and I am glad I did! Tending the horses may not pay as well as some things, but I have made good friends here."

Others — Azuma and Gan — kept their pasts to themselves. Gan laughed outright when Baili asked about what his life had been like before he became a horse-keeper, but Azuma shook his head solemnly. "My sorrows are better left in the past, Baili-*himei*. You have enough troubles of your own to worry about without adding mine to them." Yet, despite their reticence, both men seemed to welcome Baili in their own way. Gan brought her all the palace news he could — which was much — and swore he was working on a plan to return her to her proper place. And though Azuma spoke little, he always returned Baili's tentative smiles and asked about her day each evening. By the end of the week, only Ailin still bowed and refused to look Baili in the eye — yet even she relaxed enough to converse with her.

Each morning, Baili and Chouko herded the geese from the pens to one of three shoals along the river. The geese eventually stopped attacking Baili on sight, once she became frustrated enough to shove them away as soon as they showed signs of aggression. Later in the week, Gan presented Baili with a small knife he'd found, and a simple prick of her finger allowed her to trap the birds in a net of air until they reached the river. After that, they treated her with as much resentful deference as they did Chouko. Baili walked taller all that day; even if she couldn't yet oust Lanfen, at least she could beat the geese.

Unfortunately, though the geese became less hostile, Chouko did not. She still called Baili *kuīnzuko* in a tone that made the title sound like an insult. Though she snapped orders when they worked, she refused help any time Baili offered it without being asked. Baili endured this treatment silently, but by the week's end, she realized she'd have to do more to win Chouko over.

So, one morning, once Chouko had settled down beneath a shady tree, Baili tentatively approached and bowed. "My hostess, may I ask a favor?"

Chouko did not look up. "I did not think a *kuīnzuko* would ask favors of a peasant."

"I am not much of a *kuīnzuko* just now, as you know." Baili clasped her staff in both hands. "I wondered if you would teach me your language?"

Chouko glanced up, eyebrow raised. "My language? Why?"

"Because you wished more of my people would learn it." Baili met Chouko's gaze. "And because I would like to do better than my ancestors have. I would like to greet those I meet in their own tongue, to make friends and allies rather than subjects. I know that my people have wronged yours, but perhaps it is not too late for a change."

Chouko did not reply but stared at the river, brows furrowed. Baili waited, her shoulders slowly slumping. Why had she bothered? Chouko was too stubborn, too angry, for this to work. It was hopeless.

Then Chouko spoke, her voice rough. "*Kanagi shimatsu.*"

Baili blinked. "What?"

"*Kanagi shimatsu*," Chouko repeated, facing Baili this time. "Be welcome. It is what we say when someone asks for entrance to a home or gathering."

Perhaps not so hopeless. Baili smiled and bowed again. "Thank you. How would I say that?"

"*Arishoto*." Chouko paused. "Or, speaking formally . . . *atana kanasha shimatsu.*"

"*Arishoto,* Chouko." Baili sat down next to her companion. Yes, this just might work.

The language lesson lasted all morning. By the time they stopped, Baili could greet a friend, family member, or superior — not, Chouko remarked, that she needed *that* — could say please and thank you, and could bid someone goodbye either formally or informally. Better still, Chouko no longer glowered quite so fiercely; her look conveyed more frustration than outright hatred.

They had another lesson the next morning and the morning after as well. By the third day, Chouko no longer snapped so much, nor did she spit Baili's title so bitterly. Baili almost hoped that Chouko was starting to forgive.

Then, that afternoon, a group of people appeared, walking along the river's edge. Two were palace guards, lightly armored and carrying sabers. Another was a grey-bearded man in the dark robes of a scholar. The last was a young noble garbed in richly embroidered red robes, who spoke earnestly with the old man.

When Chouko noticed the group, her eyes narrowed, and she watched them for several minutes as they neared. Then she stood and walked to the edge of the steep bank. "Baili," she called, a moment later, "come here."

Baili joined her and looked down towards the river. "What?"

Chouko pointed to a goose near the water's edge. "That one is hurt. Bring it here."

Baili took a hard look at the happily splashing goose. "Are you sure?"

"Of course." Chouko huffed. "I have been at this longer than you, *kuīnzuko*."

"Very well." Baili sighed and started carefully down the bank. But before she took two steps, something solid caught her ankle, tripping her so she tumbled down the slope with a yelp. She splashed into the water, landing facedown and dazed.

Before she could move, she heard voices call out. Several pairs of hands grasped her and pulled her into a sitting position. Baili sputtered and looked around. The nobleman's guards held her arms, and only a few paces away, on the very edge of the water, stood the nobleman himself and the old man with him.

Oh dear oh dear oh dear — Baili attempted to kneel, but movement shot pain up her left leg, so instead, she just bent as low as she could. "I — Your servant apologizes for the disturbance, my lord, and thanks you for helping her." She realized belatedly that she probably shouldn't have spoken first.

"You may rise." The nobleman didn't sound disturbed. "Do not apologize; I did only what is right, and my guards, most of that. Are you injured? Aiguo, Nian, help her from the water. She should not stay there."

The two guards obediently lifted Baili to her feet and helped her stumble to the bank. "I — thank you — I am fine — ow!" The guards released her, only for her leg to buckle. She dropped to her knees. "Do not trouble yourself about your servant."

The nobleman, taking no notice of her polite protests, knelt on the sand beside her. "Do not fear. You cannot put weight on the leg?"

"Your highness!" the old man protested. "Is it a prince's place to tend a common goose-girl? She will heal on her own."

"I know of few servants who have time for that, Master Gen." The nobleman — no, the *prince* — didn't look up. "And as you yourself have said, those given gifts are responsible to use them on behalf of their people." He addressed Baili again. "May I see the injury?"

"I — yes, of course." Baili, assisted by the guards, stretched her injured leg out in front of her. *Which prince has the healing gift? Please, Divine, let it not be Xiang!*

The prince probed her lower leg and ankle with a physician's careful touch, only the tips of his fingers touching her skin. "Your ankle is sprained only, not broken. It swells already, see? I will mend it." He drew an ornate knife from his belt and pricked his finger; just as Baili herself had done many times, and allowed a drop of blood to fall on Baili's ankle. The drop vanished, and with it, the pain. The swelling decreased, and within moments no sign of the injury remained.

The prince stood. "There. Now I must go before Master Gen decides I am overly distracted."

"I — thank you, your highness." Baili bowed as low as she could. "May the Divine's richest blessings fall upon you."

"I do only my duty." The prince smiled, then turned and walked away along the bank with his companions. Still in shock, Baili watched them go until they turned a bend. Then she recalled the goose and looked around.

It had paddled off and was happily diving for riverweed with several others. Whatever Chouko said, it certainly wasn't hurt. *What trick was she playing?* Frowning, Baili stood, located her staff, and clambered back up the bank to confront her fellow goose-girl.

CHAPTER 8

When Baili reached the top of the bank, she found Chouko sitting under a tree, smiling, smug as a cat with a mouse. "Do you know who that was, *kuīnzuko*?"

"I do not." Baili's voice came out sharper than she intended. "Nor do I know why I was tripped going down to fetch a goose that needed no fetching. I beg you, O honored hostess, enlighten me."

Chouko's eyebrows rose, one arching slightly higher than the other, but she recovered quickly. "That was his highness Prince Liu Xiang, eldest son and heir of the emperor, betrothed of the princess of Seven Rivers. And that should answer your other question as well."

Oh, Divine help me. It was *him.* Baili shut her eyes in exasperation and embarrassment. "No, *gracious hostess*, it does not. Forgive my ignorance, for surely I am a lowly fool compared to you, but I do not see why his presence should make you *nearly kill* your fellow worker."

"All know his highness's gift is to make the broken whole." Chouko still smirked, undaunted. "He will heal anyone injured or ill, even the lowest beggar. And in healing you, he noticed you and now will not forget you."

"What good does it for him to notice a goose girl?" Baili clutched her staff, half-tempted to whack Chouko over the head. "In my current state, I am nothing to him, as you continuously point out that *all* of *us* animal keepers are to the nobility!"

"Perhaps." Chouko shrugged. "But you are the fairest nothing of all, and that counts for something. If nothing else, his highness may wonder why a goose girl is more beautiful than his most beautiful of brides."

"Perhaps." Baili had herself wondered how Lanfen would convince anyone that she was the fairest in the land. "But if I had been hurt beyond the prince's capacity to heal? What of that?"

"People say that his highness can heal anyone who breathes. And he will *try*, simply to see if they are right." Chouko leaned forward, her eyes glinting. "You cannot claim what is yours without risk. Are you too much of a *kuīnzuko* to accept that risk yourself?"

"I am not *asking* to be treated as a *kuīnzuko*! I am asking to be treated as a human being!" Baili clenched both hands around her staff. A breeze swept over the water's surface, flowing around Baili and into Chouko's face. The geese honked and hissed and clustered into angry, frightened groups, looking for something to attack. "Would you have done the same to — to Gan, were he in my place? To Ailin? Or Jialin? Or Azuma? Or any of the others? Would you?"

Chouko stood, clutching her own staff, shoulders back and eyes wide, but still defiant. "They would not need me to do it."

"*Pretend.*" Baili met Chouko's defiance with her own, the wind lending her courage. "I think you would not."

"Fine. No. But tell me, *kuīnzuko* —" Chouko's anger raged like a storm across her face — "If you met one who had taken everything from you, who had treated your kinfolk as prizes and slaves, what would you do? What would you *not* do?"

"I wouldn't do as you have!" Baili snapped. "I wouldn't almost kill them over a grudge, justified or not!"

"Would you not?" Chouko demanded "Your history says otherwise. Who razed *Sorashima* after her ruler refused a treaty that would have practically enslaved his people? Who killed an entire clan over a supposed insult by their leader? Who burned *Kasenotoshi*; who conquers everything; who takes the best of the *Kasai Shotō* and leaves her remaining people to struggle? Who sows destruction at a hint of rebellion, yet never lifts a finger when clan wars kill hundreds?

"Your people. Your *family*." Chouko pinned Baili with her glare. "So, *kuīnzuko*, can you truly say you would not act as I? You, who even now call wind and water to threaten me though I did you no real harm?"

Baili opened her mouth to shoot back a reply — then stopped. *This isn't helping.* Chouko carried enough anger of her own without Baili to fuel the flame. With effort, Baili stilled the wind and relaxed her grip on her staff. "Perhaps not. I do not deny, never have denied, that you and yours have many grievances against me and mine. We have treated you as prizes, not people, and we were wrong to do so. But *I* have not, nor have I asked for special treatment, only to be treated as another person and given a chance to right my ancestors' wrongs. I ask that again now."

"So you say." Chouko was shaking now, whether in sorrow or anger, Baili wasn't sure. "But what guarantee have I that you will remember your promise when you sit in splendor and I am still here tending geese?"

"You have the witness of my actions. And you have my word, not on my ancestors' tarnished honor, but on my own, still being shaped. I swear to you, I will remember." Baili bowed her head. "I can offer no more; will you accept what I have as enough?"

Chouko hesitated several long moments. "It is accepted. But do not neglect your promises."

"I will not." Baili smiled hesitantly. "Perhaps we could start again on a clean slate, honored hostess?"

"Perhaps." Chouko nodded. "And perhaps, as we do, you could call me my own name."

"I should like that." Baili bent low as if greeting a foreign dignitary. "*Anata ni shukufu*, Nakahara Chouko."

Chouko bowed back, more deeply. "*Anata ni shukufu*, Baili." She straightened. "Perhaps we do not tell Gan of this?"

Baili also stood and nodded. "Agreed. He will not hear of it."

"Good." Chouko smiled almost teasingly. "And next time his highness appears, I will not push you in the river."

Baili tilted her head. "Next time?"

"He noticed you, as I said, and he will not forget the fairest nothing in the land." Chouko's smile became sharp. "Be sure, he will return soon."

CHAPTER 9

Three days passed with no sign of the prince, but Chouko stuck to her prediction all the same. Baili didn't press the subject. Since their argument, Chouko had been making a clear effort to be less hostile, and Baili didn't want to risk that peace. Their language lessons helped. Chouko still snapped occasionally when Baili stumbled over a phrase for the ninth or tenth time, but she seemed to appreciate Baili's determination to learn all the same.

Then, on the fourth day, a newcomer appeared on the path along the riverbank. "A hunter?" Baili guessed when she spotted him, noting his sturdy garb and the short bow and quiver on his back. "That seems odd." How much game could there be along the goose pastures.

"*Hantū*," Chouko translated automatically before she followed Baili's gaze and spotted the man as well. A slow, smug smile spread across her face. "Or not a *hantū*. Look again, *kuīnzuko*."

Baili did, wondering why. Then the man happened to glance up so she could see his face beneath his wide straw hat. Her eyes widened, and her breath caught. *Oh, Divine . . .* This man was indeed not a hunter, nor even a stranger, for Baili had met him only a few days earlier when he wore royal robes and knelt on the riverbank beside her.

Prince Xiang had returned.

Chouko gave Baili a significant look. "See, *kuīnzuko*? What did I say?"

"I know." Baili turned to watch the prince out of the corner of her eye. "You were right."

"Of course." Chouko smiled smugly, but she fell silent as the prince climbed up the slope towards them.

He made a perfunctory bow and addressed them. "Ladies, I have lost my waterskin. Would one of you kindly give your humble servant a drink?"

Chouko nudged Baili, rather harder than necessary. Baili stood, picking up her waterskin, and bowed back. "It would be my pleasure, sir."

She offered him the waterskin. He took it and drank deeply. "I thank you, maiden. May I ask your name?"

"I am called Baili, sir." Baili kept her head slightly bowed. "May I know yours as well?"

"I am called Xiang." He handed the waterskin back, smiling. "You share a name with the foreign princess?"

"Indeed. I was born in her country." Baili glanced up to catch his reaction, hoping he would understand.

"I see." The prince nodded. "The day is hot, Baili-*shán,* and a hunter has little companionship, certainly none so fair as you. May I join you for a time?"

"Of course, Xiang-*rón.*" Baili bowed again. "My friend and I would be glad for your company. Will you sit?"

"Gladly, thank you." Xiang seated himself by the tree. As he did, Chouko stood and, with an annoyed outburst in her language, stalked towards the river.

Baili tried to smile even as her cheeks grew warm. "Um. My friend has noticed an injured goose and regrets that she must go see to it."

"Ah." Xiang's eyebrows rose. "She is a foreigner? Her language is strange indeed, that regret sounds so much like anger."

"It is much like our own, honored sir; much of the meaning is in the delivery." Baili sat by Xiang, careful to keep a proper distance between them. "And I may have interpreted incorrectly; I began learning only a week ago so that she and I might understand each other while we work."

"I do not doubt that you translate well." Xiang pushed back his hat so it sat on the back of his head. "If you will not think your servant forward, Baili-*shán,* may I ask why a maiden of the Kingdom of Seven Rivers keeps geese for the emperor of the Kingdom of Three Peaks?"

"You may ask, and your servant is glad to answer." Baili folded her hands in her lap, rapidly choosing details to share. "My honored parents joined my ancestors in *Shénme Jíang* many years ago. Before then, they arranged my marriage to a young man of this kingdom, whose ancestors were of old both

57

friends and enemies of my family. I traveled here to wed him, but my attendants turned against me on the road and left me for dead. I reached the city alone only to find that my betrothed had been tricked into binding himself to another. With nowhere else to turn, I found work and shelter here."

"I see." Xiang nodded gravely. "Could you not have approached your betrothed's family and revealed the deception?"

"Perhaps, sir," Baili replied, "yet the deceiver's trickery was such that I feared for my life should I speak. And so I have trusted the Divine to show me another way to set all to rights or else place me in a better future than my honored parents planned."

"I shall pray when I visit my family's altar that He will do as you hope, Baili-*shán*." Xiang shook his head. "It is unfortunate that so many good men and women are afflicted in their marriages, for I have similar troubles. My honored parents arranged my betrothal to a lovely woman from afar, whom I had met on few occasions but greatly admired whenever I saw her. Yet when my bride-to-be arrived at my father's home, I found her little like what I remembered."

So Xiang suspected Lanfen was not who she claimed! Baili struggled to hide her elation. "That is most unfortunate, Xiang-*rón*. As you have promised to pray for me, so I shall also pray for you, that the truth may be revealed soon."

"My thanks to you." Xiang glanced at the sky. "But the noon hour passes and I am keeping you from your lunch. Will you forgive your servant his rudeness?"

"What is there to forgive, honored sir?" Baili shook her head. "To sit with you is as pleasant as the finest banquet."

"You honor me, fair maiden," Xiang replied with a smile. "May I then join you at your meal? If not, say the word and your humble servant will depart at once ere he causes a lady to faint for lack of nourishment."

Baili blushed, fiddling with the fabric of her skirt. "I am a mere goose girl, sir. I have no lunch from which to be kept. Yet if you wish to go, let not this humble maiden stop you."

"Ah. Oh." Xiang, temporarily lost for words, recovered gallantly. "Forgive your servant his presumption. Will you honor him by allowing him to share his meal with you — and your friend, of course, if she wishes?"

She should say no. That would be proper. A man and a woman shouldn't eat together alone unless they were married . . .

Or betrothed. And Baili and Xiang were that, even if Lanfen had come between them. So this was confirmation that Xiang knew who she was and believed her story! Smiling giddily, Baili bowed until her nose nearly touched her skirts. "Your servant would be delighted. Allow me to ask Chouko if she wishes to join us also." She stood and hurried over to her companion.

Chouko raised an eyebrow at Baili's approach and made a sarcastic-sounding comment in her language. Baili ignored it. "Xiang-*rón* has offered to share his meal with us. Do you want some?"

Chouko snorted and spoke quietly. "I did not push you down a hill and play the fool so I could share a meal with two lovers. And I certainly want none of *his* food." She pointed at Baili. "To share a table with you is one thing. When you first ate with me, you were a wanderer in need, and now you are a *yujinaijin*, same as Gan. This man is neither. Go eat; I will be fine without." Raising her eyebrow, she added, "Besides, listening to you two attempt to flirt is annoyance enough. Watching would put me off my food completely."

Baili blushed. "We are not —"

"He is." Chouko waved a hand. "Go. Enjoy your lunch. Win back your man."

CHAPTER 10

That evening, when Baili and Chouko told the others of the day's events, Gan laughed proudly. "Hah! I knew that man would not be fooled by a pretty face when there is a prettier one nearby. He has looked and found truth, just as I planned."

"As *you* planned, Ganbaatar?" Chouko set down her chopsticks and glared across the table. "I recall no plans from *you*."

"Do not blame Gan, Chouko. I began it," Ailin said meekly. "I told him that we should not leave his highness's learning of our guest to chance."

"She echoed my thoughts, and when two think alike, that is reason for action." Gan smirked. "We were no fools, *erveekei*. On the *günja's* first day here, we listened to the winds, Ailin in the kitchens and I in the stables. All news finds one or the other in time. And when the winds whispered that the prince was delaying every ceremony and that he and his father secretly doubted the river princess, we started our own breezes."

"And we succeeded." Ailin smiled, looking down at her bowl as if embarrassed by her pride. "There are a dozen rumors now, spread all through the castle, court, and city, but not one is in the false princess's favor."

"Indeed." Nianzu leaned forward. "The widest-spread one is simply the false princess's story turned on its head, that she is in truth the cousin who, out of jealousy, charmed all the guards into turning against the princess, but failed to kill her and so concocted her tale as protection."

Baili smiled. "Oh? Then anyone who knows that rumor almost knows the truth."

"So they do, but what of it?" Chouko snorted. "Only a fool acts on mere rumor."

"That is not true." As Baili thought through all the implications of Gan's plan, her smile grew. "The common people hear the rumors and distrust the false princess, but will welcome me when I step forward. As for the court, any noble knows that rumor holds a grain of truth. Most have servants tasked with keeping track of gossip and finding the truth behind it. They will hear the first story, look deeper, and discover what we know. And the prince himself, if already suspicious, would see the rumors as an excuse to investigate further."

"And what of the false princess?" Chouko pointed her chopsticks at Gan. "If his highness has heard of this, she surely has as well. What happens when she learns where the rumors started?

"Do not fear, Chouko." Baili shook her head. "Until the wedding, Lanfen remains a guest in the emperor's house. She cannot simply have people killed as she wishes. Imprisoned, perhaps, or brought before the emperor, but if the emperor is suspicious, neither would be so dangerous as before." Baili's smile faded. "If she does act, it will be in the night and against me alone. Without a noble's support, you cannot speak against her, and explaining the deaths of four or eight people, even animal keepers, would be difficult."

"You are not wrong, *günja*, though she may grow paranoid and strike anyway." Gan shook his head gravely. "But I will know before she acts. The emperor and his court are not the only ones with eyes and ears in many places."

"How?" Baili asked. "You are —" She broke off, not wishing to offend. "You do not have a noble's resources."

"Ah. 'Ganbaatar is only a keeper of horses, what can he do?' Is that your thought, *günja*?" Gan crossed his arms, raising his chin proudly. "So he is, but he is owed favors, and he owes favors to those who want to be repaid, and every Plainsman in the city answers to him, even those who have never known the plains."

"Then why are you still here?" Nianzu demanded. "With such connections, you could have escaped long ago!"

Gan shrugged. "So I could. Perhaps one day I will. But I am the tenth son of my father, neither eldest nor youngest, and will find no great honor or work among my own people save in battle. Yet here I am a leader who serves many peoples. What better honor or work could I find?" He leveled a stern look at Baili. "Understand, *günja*; I tell you this so you know you are safe. If you use this knowledge wrongly later, you shall soon regret it. Plainsmen look after their own."

Baili bowed her head with a smile. "I thank you for your trust, Gan. I think that I owe you many favors already, and if I seek you out again after this is over, it shall surely be that I may owe you more."

"Hah! That is well, then!" Gan smirked at Chouko. "See, *erveekei*? This one, she trusts me, as should you."

"'This one' has not been entangled in some of your previous schemes." Chouko huffed and picked a piece of water chestnut from her bowl. "You say 'all is well,' but I see much risk."

"Nonsense." Gan waved a hand dismissively. "A week from this day, our *günja* will sit at feast beside her prince and the false princess will wail in the dungeons. Wait and see."

~~~~~~

For a few days, Baili thought Gan might be right. Xiang visited each day, bringing with him meals to share. As they ate, they spoke in veiled terms of their lives and experiences and in plain words of themselves and their dreams. Yet as the days passed with no trouble, they grew steadily bolder in their conversation, and at last Xiang brought up Bloodgifts. "I have always wondered," he said, sitting with his back to a tree and his fingers woven through Baili's, "about the princess's gift. Control of air is not uncommon in the Liu line, but command of water is."

"Oh?" Baili half-turned so she could properly see Xiang's face. "What do you wonder?"

"Many things. If it is difficult to control. If she must touch the water to bend it to her will. What she can command it to do." Xiang's gaze wandered down the mountain and towards the palace for a moment. "I have heard that the prince has asked the princess in the palace to demonstrate more than once, but she has always begged weariness."

"Very strange." Baili hesitated a moment, then gave Xiang what she hoped was a coy smile. "Would you like to see the princess's gift now?"

Xiang turned to face her, all seriousness save for the spark of curiosity in his eyes. "If she deems it safe, her servant would be honored."

"Who is here to see but the geese and Chouko and you?" Baili pulled her hand out of Xiang's and slid her knife out of the pocket of her robe. She pricked her finger, squeezed out several drops of blood, and then drew together the water in the air to form a sphere above her hand. With another thought and a flick of her fingers, the water flowed into the shape of a dragon which circled her hand and then flew upwards until it burst into a shower of droplets.

Xiang blinked as one of the droplets hit him in the nose. "Amazing." He turned his attention back to Baili, keeping his voice low. "You do not have to touch the water, then?"

"Only sometimes. If I wished to control the river — to create waves or currents or such — I would have to touch it. But I can control the water in the air without touch, perhaps because I control the air itself as well and so it is like I am still touching it." Baili wiped away the remaining blood onto the grass. "So what do you think of the princess's gift?"

"I think it is as lovely as she is." Xiang took Baili's hand once more. "And I hope that sometime, I shall see it again."

"You will. When —" A goose's honk and the sound of voices on the path above interrupted her. Baili ducked her head but watched out of the corner of her eye as a group of soldiers passed by. She thought she saw Captain Zhihao among them — but perhaps that was only her imagination.

Neither Baili nor Xiang spoke again until the group was gone. Only then did Baili realize how tightly she'd been clutching Xiang's hand. She loosened her grip, blushing and took a deep breath. "You will see it again. But, I think, not today."

Xiang nodded, watching the direction the soldiers had disappeared. "Not today indeed." He glanced back at her and smiled reassuringly. "Do not fear, Baili-*shán*. A little longer and all shall be well."

Baili nodded silently. *Please, Divine, let that be true.*

CHAPTER 11

Three days after Baili demonstrated her Bloodgift, Xiang brought her a sketchbook and charcoal pencils, which she accepted gratefully. Chouko scoffed at the gift, even after Baili explained: "It is traditional for grooms-to-be to give their brides pen and paper, or silk and thread, or clay and paint, anything which can be used to create. Then the first thing the bride makes, she gives back to him. It shows that he will provide for both her desires and her needs and that she will not hoard his provision for herself."

"It is a rich man's tradition," Chouko replied archly, eyeing the pencils. "Who but the wealthy can waste time on such things?" With that, she stalked off towards the river.

Baili ignored Chouko's comment, instead reveling in her art. And however Chouko felt about Xiang, she didn't complain when he brought Baili exotic fruit to share with the other animal keepers. Eventually, she even unbent her pride enough to converse a few minutes with him, with Baili as "translator."

Then, just a week later, the news arrived. Ailin, pale-faced, told them first: rumors among the kitchen staff said that Empress Zhu Yawen was coming to Three Peaks to attend her stepdaughter's wedding. The next day, over dinner, Gan confirmed Ailin's words: Yawen was on her way and would arrive in two weeks.

Chouko scowled at Gan. "Did I not warn you? See what has come upon us! An empress may have all our heads if she pleases."

"Do not blame Gan." Baili looked down at her lap. "I should have thought of this myself. The empress has the Dragonglass. Surely when she received Lanfen's report, she consulted the glass and discovered my situation" She sighed, shoulders slumping. "I am truly sorry for putting you all in danger. I never meant to. Perhaps if I left —"

"Where would you go?" Azuma asked quietly. "Are you ready to reclaim your place?"

Baili sighed. "No. The time is not yet right; I must have indisputable proof of my identity — something more than my Bloodgift — before I act. For the security of my and Xiang's future, I must dispel all doubt of who I am." She paused. "In that respect, the empress brings one hope with her. She will carry the Dragonglass, and if I can somehow access that, I can use it to prove myself."

Azuma raised an eyebrow. "That will require you to get quite close to the empress."

"I know." Baili swallowed hard. "Perhaps I can sneak in after she arrives, or if worst comes to worst, I will go to the palace, appeal to the emperor, and hope for the best." She looked around the table. "Yet if I stay, I will be in danger, and all of you with me. Perhaps, if I cannot leave, Gan could help you escape before the empress arrives. You could return to your homes or go elsewhere. I would ask Xiang for any aid he might be able to provide you as well. I know it would be difficult, but at least you would be alive."

"The Riders of the Plains do not flee, *günja*." Gan crossed his arms. "Not when those who depend on them cannot. There are many who look to me, and if I leave, how will I return? If it comes to the worst, some in this city will hide me; perhaps they will hide you as well. But a Rider does not leave his people without their leader and he does not leave a friend defenseless when storms lurk at the sky's edge." He gestured to the others. "Any here who wish to go, I will have to safety within a week. But this Rider remains here."

"I will not go." Ailin's gaze stayed fixed on the table, but her voice was firm. "Baili-*xiá* is my princess, and I will stay with her until she bids me leave."

"I'll stay as well," Nianzu said. "I have helped Gan this far. I will see his plans through."

"We will also stay." Renshu indicated Jialin and himself. "Where else could we go? With so many newcomers from Seven Rivers, we have small chance elsewhere. Better to risk our lives for something worthwhile than to beg in relative safety. Unless Jialin disagrees?"

Jialin shook her head. "Renshu is all I have left in this world. Where he goes, I go."

"Hah! So only the Fire Islanders remain." Gan turned to Azuma and Chouko. "What say you? I

69

cannot promise you your homeland, but I can perhaps set you on your way. Will you leave us?"

For once, Azuma spoke first. "No. I fought for a princess's honor once before. She was the last ruler of her clan; I, one of the last of her guards." He shifted, sat straighter. "She is gone now, but here is another princess who needs my protection, and I will fight for her as I did my own."

Baili shook her head and smiled in disbelief. "You do me great honor, sir. How did I earn such loyalty?"

"By who you are, what you represent, Baili-*himei*." Azuma paused. "And, too, I think my princess would want me to do this."

All eyes turned to Chouko, who huffed and tossed her head like a wild horse caught in a pen. "Better that Gan should send me to his homeland, not my own. The Fire Islands are my land, but I have no future there while clan wars still rage. In Gan's land, perhaps I could be free to do as I please and fear no man. But if the rest of you remain, I will not play the coward. Someone must temper your heroics. And —" her gaze slid towards Baili. "If the *kuīnzuko* survives, as I hope she will, I wish to see her promises kept, but in order to do that, she will need more protection than Gan and Azuma and the geese."

Baili's smile widened. "Thank you, Chouko-*koyū*. I am honored to have you at my side."

"Thank me by remembering your promises." But Chouko smiled as well, a rare, real smile. "You are a brave *kuīnzuko*. Foolish, but brave. I am glad to have known you."

"And I, you." Baili glanced around the hut and silently gave thanks. Perhaps with such companions by her side and Xiang and the emperor willing to listen, she stood a chance against Yawen and Lanfen.

CHAPTER 12

The news that Empress Yawen was on her way to the Kingdom of Three Peaks sent Baili into a spiral of nervous tension. Logically, she knew that she was in no more danger now than she had been a week ago; the real peril would not begin until near Yawen's arrival. Yet logic didn't stop her from checking her knife every time someone passed on the paths along the river or above the goose-pastures, or from jumping any time she heard a raised voice or even a goose's alarmed honk.

As the first week after Gan's announcement dragged past, Xiang's daily visits became Baili's sole respite. True, she had evenings in the hut, where she felt almost safe, surrounded as she was by friends, but undercurrents of uncertainty simmered in every conversation. Gan and Azuma debated strategies for deposing Lanfen before Yawen's coming or getting the Dragonglass once the empress arrived, but every idea had too many holes for anything but a last-ditch effort.

With Xiang, however, there, was no talk of plans or strategies or danger or prophecy. At times they danced around the topic, drawn to it and yet wary, like moths that fluttered at the edges of a flame but dared not come too close. Those occasions were rare, though, and mostly they discussed happier things: fond memories of the past, dreams of the future, odd thoughts they each had over the course of the day. Once, Xiang asked Baili what she would do if she could do anything, if she had no responsibilities or restrictions to hold her back. Baili thought for only a few minutes before replying: "I would find a boat and a crew to man her, and sail down the river and out to the sea and find a beautiful place I have never seen before, somewhere peaceful and safe. I would stay there for a time, and then I would return home and sit in my garden and remember my adventure. And you?"

Xiang laughed. "I would spend days on end in the forest, returning to my home only by night to eat by my own fireside. And I would walk among the people of the city and the country without fear of what will happen if I say the wrong thing or aid the wrong person. But that will never happen." He squeezed her hand, which he held in his. "Yet, Baili-*shán*, for you, one day I will hire a craft and captain and take you to find your beautiful, peaceful place across the sea. Wait and see."

From there, their conversation moved on to other things: to Baili's sketches and the deer Xiang saw in the forest that day and the antics of the geese in the river. They were small things, almost meaningless, but made meaningful by the sharing. And as long as they talked, Baili felt safe: protected physically by Xiang and Chouko and the geese, and protected in her heart by Xiang's desire to know her, not as a princess or as the fulfillment of prophecy, but as just Baili.

It was bliss. And so, of course, it couldn't last. A week and a day after Baili learned of Yawen's plans, as Xiang bowed farewell to her, he said, "I fear, Baili-*shán*, that I shall not be able to visit you like this again for a little while."

"Oh?" Baili clasped her hands. She already knew what he was going to say, yet she prayed she was wrong. "I am sorry to hear that; my days will be far duller without your presence to brighten them."

"And mine far sadder without your smile to cheer them. But —" Xiang paused. "May I speak openly, my lady?"

Baili nodded. "Yes, but do so softly. Is this to do with the empress's coming?"

"Indeed." Xiang lowered his voice and leaned in close, smiling in a way that matched neither words nor tone. "You already know?"

Baili nodded, forcing a smile as well. "One of my companions told me a week ago, when he first received the news."

"Then you understand the danger." Xiang grasped both of Baili's hands and looked her in the eyes. "I do not wish to leave you here, but I fear what will happen should the empress find you. I hoped to bring you to court and reveal the truth before she arrived, but the time is not yet right. And if the empress demands so-called justice . . . it is harder to refuse an empress than a princess. You understand? I do not wish to lead her to you by accident."

"I understand." Baili bowed her head. "I will be careful, and my friends will keep me safe. Do not fear for me." She hesitated — *Do I tell him?* Yes. He needed to know. "Be wary of the empress, my lord. You know of the prophecy?" She waited for Xiang's nod before she continued. "I may be the fairest, but she was before me, and she believes she is better suited to carry out what was foretold. She wishes that the kingdoms be united not merely by treaty but under her rule. I beg you, do not allow this to happen. My own land has suffered under her reign, as you doubtless know. I would not see the same fate befall your land and people, especially not when so many of my own have come here seeking respite."

"I will be wary. Empress Yawen will harm neither my kingdom nor my bride if I may prevent it." Xiang let go of Baili's hand long enough to nudge her chin back up so he could meet her eyes once more. "Do not fear. I will return when I can, and I hope that when next I see you, I will be able to restore what is yours. Until then, be watchful. If it is safe, I will try to send something near noon each day; I do not wish you to sit hungry."

"I thank you, my lord." Baili managed a real smile this time. "But do not worry for me. See to the empress and your kingdom. That is most important."

"The life of my bride is no less important than my kingdom." Xiang looked down at their clasped hands. "May I kiss your hand before I go?"

Baili blushed. "You may." And so Xiang bent and pressed his lips to the back of her hand. Then he departed with a final bow and a look that said he longed to stay.

If that first week had been torture, the next week was worse. Baili knew Yawen could arrive at any time now, if the message had been slowed or if her company crossed the mountains more swiftly than Baili's had. The conversation around the table in the hut became more urgent, yet not even Gan had any new ideas. Baili prayed that Xiang and his father had some plan in mind, since she and her friends were getting nowhere.

The number of passers-by on the river and road increased as well. Many of them looked suspiciously soldier-like, and Baili suspected Xiang had sent them in secret to watch over her. And indeed, at some point each day, one of the passers-by would stop to greet her and Chouko and would offer them a wrapped packet of food, saying it was from a hunter friend. The meals were solid, simple affairs, but they always included fruit, sometimes exotic, sometimes not. No matter what food was sent, Chouko insisted on tasting everything before Baili ate, saying that Gan would never let her rest if Baili died of poison.

Then, one day, it didn't matter anymore.

~~~~~

"Ah! Oh my!" The high, cracked voice, accompanied by a cacophony of thumps, pulled Baili's attention from the road to the riverbank. Her hand fell to her hidden knife, but then she relaxed. A stooped woman in a worn black robe and straw hat had tripped and now tried to gather round red fruits that must have fallen from the basket on her back.

Baili stood, grasping her staff. "We should go help her. She is only an old woman, no danger to us." She hurried down the slope, calling, "Honored mother, may we aid you?" Chouko followed, muttering something about traps.

The woman struggled to her feet as Baili approached. "Ah, thank you, child. Will you help an old woman gather her apples? My knees will not let me crawl about as I once did." Her voice sounded familiar, yet Baili couldn't place it.

"Gladly, honored mother." Baili bent to collect the scattered fruit.

"Hmph. Next time, old one, take the city road so you will not stumble." Grumbling, Chouko waded into the river shallows to fetch the apples there. "How did you come by these? I would look for them in the emperor's kitchens, not on a grandmother's back."

"It is to the emperor's kitchens I bring them." The old woman stiffly swung the basket off her shoulders, keeping her head bowed. "Years ago, a lost merchant traded apple seeds from the distant west for bed and dinner. Now I bring my first crop to the emperor in honor of the prince's marriage."

"Ah." Baili dropped the apples into the basket. *Perhaps the same merchant brought my family our seeds.* She remembered seeing fruit like this on some of the trees in the orchards. "That is good of you, honored mother. May he receive your gifts with gladness."

"And may you be blessed for your kindness to a poor old woman." The lady turned the basket to Chouko. "May I offer you each an apple as thanks?"

Chouko shook her head emphatically, adding her load to those in the basket. "I will not take food meant for the emperor's table. Go your way, grandmother, and be careful where you step."

"As you will." The old woman bowed, then seemed to notice the geese. "But — ah! You are the girls who keep the emperor's geese?"

"Perhaps, yes." Chouko crossed her arms. "What of it?"

The woman inspected her apples and picked out two. "Earlier this day, a young hunter helped me when my boat sprang a leak. Like you, he refused any reward, but told me of a pretty girl and a foreigner who tend the emperor's geese. He asked that if I passed them, I should give each an apple on his behalf. So, will you take his gift, if not mine?"

Baili looked at Chouko. "If they are from him . . ."

"Hmph. Very well." Chouko held out a hand. "We accept."

"Good." The woman handed an apple first to Baili, then to Chouko. "Will you do an old woman another favor? Try them now and tell me how you like them."

Chouko opened her mouth, probably to refuse, but Baili nodded. "Of course." Without hesitation, she bit into the fruit. Juicy sweetness filled her mouth as she chewed and swallowed. "This is good! Try it, Chouko!" She took another bite before the sweetness turned sour and her throat and mouth began to burn. "What —?" she coughed and gasped for air as her throat tightened.

Chouko dropped her untouched apple and sprang across the path to Baili's side as Baili fell to her knees. "You fool! Don't talk! Cough it up if you can."

Baili tried to obey, willing the fruit to come back up and take the burning with it. But instead she choked, and grey clouded her vision. Chouko's voice seemed to come from a long way off. She glimpsed the old woman's face beneath her hat and thought she looked familiar. *Where have I seen her before? Someone . . . someone from home . . .*

The pieces clicked. *Yawen! In disguise! No!* Baili tried to scream, to warn Chouko. But breath failed her, and the grey in her vision turned to black. Then she knew no more.

CHAPTER 13

Stillness surrounded her.

For a long time, there had been no stillness, only fire and pain. But now all was black save for thin threads of grey, stretched to breaking, that kept her from floating down a current towards a pearly glow.

Then came a *jolt.* Her heart leapt, worked furiously as if to make up for its formerly sluggish pace. The stillness shattered; the threads became ropes. She felt warmth at her side, rough robes against her skin. A murmur of voices surrounded her, and the now-familiar scents of dirt, animals, and vegetable broth filled her nose, along with another smell, something clean and rich and elegant.

Baili forced her eyes open and stared into the face of Prince Liu Xiang as he bent over her. He hastily pulled back, schooling his expression to royal composure. "Your highness. Princess Baili. It gladdens me to see you awake."

"I — um —" Baili blinked. *I . . . I was in the field? And then — Yawen! She must have poisoned me*

. . . But now I'm in the hut? And Xiang is here? How? What of Chouko? "What happened?"

Off to the side, Chouko snorted. "You nearly died is what happened. I had to fight off a fire-cursed bloodwitch and drag you all the way here."

Baili pushed herself into a sitting position, ignoring the pain in her head, and stared at Chouko. "You fought off my stepmother? On your own? Are you —?"

"She was your stepmother? The empress?" Chouko considered this and smiled fiercely. "Yes. I did. And from that fight, I learned that her blood is poison, and that is why the apple nearly killed you. But she is no terrible foe. With my staff and the geese, I chased her off easily enough."

Baili blinked again, then burst out laughing. "Oh, Chouko-*koyū*, if only I had seen!" Her laughs turned to coughs, after which she added, "And then you went to his highness?"

Gan, seated at the table, shook his head. "No. Then she brought you here and, once you were safe, came to *me*."

"And Master Ganbaatar passed along a message warning me that my bride was dying and that I should meet him at a certain place in order to save her," Xiang finished. "And so here we are."

"But where next?" Gan crossed his arms. "You cannot wait longer, prince of peaks. Not to claim justice for your lady would be an honorless act, worthy only of a horseless fool."

"If you believe I will sit idle, you have been ill-informed of my character." Xiang stood. "The empress will surely arrive officially tomorrow

81

morning. I have in mind that we confront her then. Princess Baili shall spend the night in the palace and will join us tomorrow as a lady of the court, ready to speak when the moment is right. A few of you shall attend her: Gan and another of his choosing as her guards, and Chouko and another chosen by the princess as maids in waiting. Chouko must come, as only she witnessed the attack." He raised an eyebrow. "Thankfully, she has mastered our language in a remarkably short time."

Chouko tilted her chin defiantly and smirked. "We of the Fire Isles must be quick learners to survive our conquerors. But what voice does a foreign servant have in the emperor's court?"

"The voice I say she has." Xiang met her gaze squarely. "And if you speak truth, Nakahara Chouko, I will see that you are not silenced, either now or in the future."

Chouko huffed. "Why should I speak otherwise?"

Baili raised a hand, hoping to forestall further argument. "Chouko-*koyū*, will you help me up?" Chouko did, pulling Baili to her feet and allowing her to lean on her shoulder. Baili faced Xiang. "Chouko and Ailin will attend me tomorrow, but I wish that all seven of my companions stay within the palace tonight."

Xiang frowned. "As you wish, but must all come? I will set guards here to protect the others."

Baili tightened her grip on Chouko's shoulder, forcing herself to speak firmly despite her instinct to submit. *Divine, please, help me. If I cannot stand for my friends now, how can I speak for their peoples later?* "I know my stepmother, Prince Xiang. She knows that Chouko lives and may have told others what happened. She will not risk the tale spreading further. I do not know if she will strike tonight, but I wish my friends to be safe." With her free hand, she gestured around the hut. "They would stand with me in danger, but I would not have them at risk unnecessarily. Do we agree?"

Xiang bowed slightly. "Very well, princess. Come, and bring your friends. I will see that you have food and safe lodging in the palace. Then we will discuss our plans."

~~~~~

The next morning, Baili stood in the throne room along with the rest of the court. Xiang had positioned her near the dais where he sat with his family, close enough that they could catch each other's eyes every so often. There she waited, fidgeting with the wide sleeves of her silk robe. Just behind her stood Ailin and Chouko, dressed in linen in Baili's colors. Ailin appeared the picture of a humble maidservant: attentive but composed, her head bowed and hands folded. Chouko, on the other hand, stood straight as a soldier, studying the court accusingly. Against the wall were Gan and Azuma in light, formal armor borrowed from the palace armory.

Baili glanced towards the dais. The emperor sat on his golden seat, the empress consort on his left, Xiang on his right. A tapestry behind him displayed his crest: three mountains, a sun, and a flame. And at the edge of the dais, directly across from Baili, stood Lanfen with her two attendants, Captain Zhihao, and a half-dozen guards, watching the throne room doors anxiously.

A gong sounded and those great doors swung inwards. A herald announced, "Her imperial majesty, Zhu Yawen, Empress of the Kingdom of Seven Rivers."

The empress swept in, attended by guards and servants, her red and gold robes flowing, dark hair held up by golden combs, jewels flashing on forehead, throat, and fingers. The faintest dusting of snowy powder hid the age marks on her face, and red paint accented her lips and the corners of her eyes.

Baili and the court bowed as the empress strode past to the dais. There, she in turn bowed her head. "Emperor Liu Yijun, I thank you for the honor you show me and my court in welcoming us. May the Divine bless this visit and bring from it a new age of friendship between our lands."

Emperor Yijun rose and returned the gesture. "And we welcome you, Empress Zhu Yawen, to our land. May this meeting bring fortune to both our empires."

Xiang also stood and bowed. "Indeed, as my honored father has said, welcome. I am pleased to meet again the mother of my bride. Your daughter has also come to welcome you; will you greet her?"

"Of course." Yawen smiled coolly. "I have missed my stepdaughter this past month."

Chouko snorted quietly. Baili held her breath as Yawen turned to Lanfen with a look far warmer than she'd ever bestowed on Baili. "My daughter, to see you brings me much pleasure."

"Not so much as your voice gives me, honored mother." Lanfen bowed, and the two embraced briefly.

The empress turned to the dais once again. "I trust that my stepdaughter has been well? I have prayed for her safety and comfort since she departed."

"She is well," Xiang replied, his face a mask, "yet for all your concern, I wonder that you do not notice that an imposter stands in your daughter's place."

The room fell suddenly, chokingly silent. Lanfen stiffened, eyes wide and lips parted, shock and anger mingled on her face. Both her and Yawen's guards reached for their sabers. Baili tensed, her fingers poised against her knife's tip. Chouko and Ailin drew closer; one of the men loosened his sword in its sheath.

Yawen lifted her head regally. "Do you claim I would not know my husband's child?"

"Do *you* take us for fools, Zhu Yawen?" Emperor Yijun folded his arms and met her gaze calmly. "No wise ruler would fail to place agents in the courts of his enemies and allies alike, nor would he receive the princess of such a court without some of those agents on hand. They all agree: this woman is not the princess but one of her handmaidens. The true princess, my son has discovered, has dwelt in hiding among my own servants since her arrival and only dared approach us after she was poisoned yesterday." The emperor gestured towards Baili. "Here stands your husband's daughter, waiting to be restored. Do you not know her?"

The empress turned, and her expression darkened. But Lanfen stepped forward, bowing deeply. "Your imperial majesty, may I speak?" He nodded, and she continued: "This is the one of whom I told you, my cousin who tried to take my place. I see that she still attempts to claim what is mine. I beg you, do not be deceived, but give her the punishment she deserves."

"Your story grew old before it was new and is the chief reason we began to doubt you," Emperor Yijun replied. "You spoke of a Gifted cousin, yet we know of no such person. Bloodgifts are not easily hidden, and we know all those who control wind and water. This cousin you describe is not among them. The princess, who you claim to be, is. Moreover, the princess is said to be strongly gifted, yet you either will not or *cannot* demonstrate any such gift."

"Emperor, allow me to explain." Yawen held up a hand. "It is true that this girl is no cousin, but rather an ignoble half-sister born near the same time, bearing a similar, but stronger, gift. Because my late husband, may his soul rest with the Divine in *Shénme Jiāng*, realized that the princess was the prophecy's fulfillment and feared for her life, he decided that the half-sister should be her decoy and appear as the princess in public, while the true princess acted as a handmaid. But it seems the girl has grown too fond of her pretended role and seeks to claim it permanently."

Whispers rippled through the court. Even Chouko muttered to herself in her own language. The emperor frowned as if considering Yawen's story; doubt flashed across Xiang's face. Baili bit her lip, trying and failing to think of an argument that Yawen couldn't twist.

Emperor Yijun spoke slowly. "If this is true, Empress Yawen, then we beg your forgiveness. Yet we knew no more of a half-sister than of a cousin, and we wish for certainty. Surely there is some proof you or they may offer which will put the matter beyond doubt?"

Baili straightened. *Now!* She stepped forward and bowed. "Your imperial majesty, I know of such a proof."

The emperor turned. "What do you propose?"

"The Dragonglass." Baili fought to keep her voice steady. "Everyone knows that the Dragonglass shows only truth, and as a princess of the Zhu line, I know that the empress must have it with her. Why should we not ask it?"

The emperor appeared to weigh the suggestion — for form's sake, Baili suspected; when she'd told Xiang her idea the night before, he promised to inform his father. "You have thought well." He turned to Yawen. "Empress Yawen, let us settle this. Bring forth the glass that we may inquire of it."

Yawen hesitated. "The Dragonglass is meant for the Zhu line alone; only they may command it. If I am to consult it, I must be alone."

"Yet both our kingdoms hang in the balance," the emperor replied. "Furthermore, both ladies should be present when their futures are decided, and we must have witnesses. The court will leave, but my son, the ladies, and I will remain, along with a few trusted attendants and guards. Is this acceptable?"

Reluctantly, Yawen bowed her head in assent. "It is."

The emperor nodded and dismissed the court and their attendants. After a few quiet words, the Three Peaks empress departed as well. Baili's companions remained, along with Lanfen's attendants and guards, and a half-dozen guards for each ruler.

The emperor and Xiang left the dais, and all gathered round Yawen, who removed the mirror from a pocket within her robes. Its silvery surface, framed by gold and jade, reflected those peering into it perfectly. Yawen glanced from Lanfen to Baili and then spoke. "Mirror of dragons, I command you: show us the princess."

The image didn't change. Xiang shook his head. "The mirror already shows the princess. Ask instead to see the true princess at some point in the past."

"Very well." Yawen cleared her throat. "Mirror of dragons, I command you, show us the princess —"

"The true princess, empress," Xiang corrected. "The true princess of the Kingdom of Seven Rivers."

Yawen gave him a cold look. "Show us the true princess of Seven Rivers three days past."

The image in the mirror rippled and a new image appeared: Baili, alone under a tree by the riverside, watching the geese. The empress frowned. Lanfen clenched her fists. Xiang smiled in triumph, while Emperor Yijun raised his eyebrows. But before any could act, Baili called, "Mirror of dragons, I command you: show us Empress Zhu Yawen when she met the princess yesterday on the riverbank."

"No —" Yawen's command came too late. The image rippled and Yawen in her disguise appeared, handing Baili an apple. The real Yawen's expression darkened, and she started to raise the mirror. "Stop."

"Mirror, let us see the whole." Baili grabbed the edge of the mirror so the empress couldn't pull it away. In the glass, her image fell, was caught by Chouko, and lay still. Chouko leapt to her feet, silently screaming at Yawen, who drew a silver dagger, pricked her finger, and spread her blood along the blade. Chouko grabbed her staff and swung, knocking Yawen into the river.

The real Yawen pulled the mirror from Baili's grasp. "You do not understand —"

"Neither the Dragonglass nor my eyes deceive me, Empress." Emperor Yijun stared her down coldly. "But you — you try to fool me with a false bride, and, worse, attempt to murder your daughter. The first I could forgive; the second, only the Divine could."

"I tried to do what is best for my kingdom." Yawen tucked the Dragonglass away, but something else shone in her hand. "I sought to save it from destruction, just as I do now." With those words, she darted forward and struck at the emperor with a knife rimmed in bright blood.

CHAPTER 14

The emperor doubled over as Yawen's knife pierced his gut. Xiang lunged forward, drawing his own weapon, but Yawen pulled back before he could strike her. She ran her finger down her blade, which was already bloodier than it had been a moment ago.

Gan drew his sword. "See to your father, highness. Leave us the empress." He, with Azuma and the emperor's guards, lunged towards her. Captain Zhihao and the empress and Lanfen's men surged forward to defend their ruler. The two forces clashed, separating Yawen, Lanfen, and Baili from Xiang and the emperor.

Chouko stooped and grabbed a spear dropped by a guard. "Run, *kuīnzuko*, Ailin. Find help. I will handle this." She darted towards Yawen, swinging the spear like a staff. "Bloodwitch! *Matsunomi*! Must you destroy your own country as well as others'?"

Yawen caught the spear just below the point. The wood immediately began to decay in her grasp. "You! You dare defy your betters again!"

Chouko jerked her staff up. The end splintered and broke, leaving a jagged point. "I defy who I will, bloodwitch, and a murderer is not my better!"

Four guards split from the group in the throne room's center. Two headed for Xiang, who'd pulled his father away from the battle and now knelt, blood dripping from his arm onto the emperor's wound. Another two ran towards Baili. Ailin grabbed Baili's sleeve. "Princess, run!"

Baili pulled free. "No. You go; fetch help. But I will run no more." With that, she drew her own knife, pushed up her sleeve, and cut her arm so blood ran towards her palm. Then she called for the wind.

It swirled past at her summons, smacking into the soldiers and knocking them off their feet. Then it rushed to wrap around the two attacking Xiang, trapping them within a cyclone of swirling air.

Baili glanced around. Gan, Azuma, and the emperor's guards were holding their own, though soldiers from both sides lay bleeding on the ground. In the center of the clash, Captain Zhihao and Gan traded swift strikes, their blades bright blurs, their armor bloody, though neither appeared wounded. Lanfen and her two attendants had disappeared. Chouko still fought Yawen, but her spear was now only an arms-length long.

The empress slashed again with her bloody dagger. Chouko blocked, but the blade sheared off the staff inches above her hands. Dropping the remainder, Chouko stumbled back and drew her own small knife.

No. Baili cut her other arm, though she'd not yet spent the blood from the first. She would need as much power as possible before the battle ended. Then, raising her hands, she drew on the wind once again until it swirled around the combatants, battering the empress and her soldiers yet merely ruffling the robes of Baili's friends.

Again she scanned the room. The emperor now sat propped up by the dais, pale but alive. Xiang stood in front of him, a knife in each hand. He nodded to her, then glanced towards Yawen. Yawen, in turn, noticed him and hissed in displeasure. She lunged towards Chouko, stabbing low. *No* — Baili split the wind; shoved Chouko out of the way. *Think.* She had to get rid of the knife — no, the blood. Yawen and her blood. That was the threat. Others could handle Yawen's soldiers as long as Yawen couldn't touch them.

Something rustled behind Baili. Baili whirled around, sending a burst of air in the direction of the sound. Lanfen stumbled back a step, clutching a dagger. She hissed and lunged forward, stabbing for Baili's stomach.

Wind slammed into Lanfen and flung her backward. The dagger flew from her grasp. Baili stepped forward, her own knife in one hand, a miniature whirlwind of air and water forming above the other. More gusts of air battered Lanfen as she scrambled back to her feet and drew another dagger.

Baili looked her former handmaiden in the eyes, and this time, she felt no fear, only determination. Lanfen would *not* be her end, not while her friends were depending on her, not when she had a purpose to fulfill. "You have one chance to run."

Lanfen hesitated, glanced from her dagger to Baili's knife and bloodied arms and the tiny storm in her hand. But not until she raised her eyes to Baili's face and find no fear there did she drop the dagger and bolt for the doors. In a matter of seconds, she was gone, no doubt trying to lose herself among the many corridors of the palace or running towards the gates and the relative safety of the road.

Baili's cuts stung. She gritted her teeth and drew the knife across her arm again as she turned back to the main battle. Now pain overwhelmed the sting, but she forced herself to flex her wrists anyway, taking in what she had missed.

She saw Captain Zhihao fall at last, run through by Gan's blade. Xiang had exchanged one of his knives for a sword and now defended his father — healed, but clearly still weakened — from another of Yawen's soldiers. Chouko, too, had found a blade, but she wielded it clumsily, barely managing to keep Yawen at bay.

This had to end now. Yawen was the key; once she was defeated, everything would be over. Baili drew in the winds from throughout the room and focused everything she had on the empress, battering her, trapping her as she had the soldiers. To the wind Baili added water, drawing it from the air so it washed away the blood on Yawen's knife and hands, and was caught in the cyclone to batter her again. One strand of wind caught Yawen's knife and spun it across the room.

The empress screamed as the wall of wind and water pressed in; screamed until water filled her mouth and choked her. She bent, dropped to her knees —

The doors burst open and imperial soldiers wearing Three Peaks colors poured in. The empress's men, seeing themselves outnumbered and their empress defeated, threw down their arms and fell prostrate. Some of the imperial warriors relieved them of the rest of their weapons and herded them into a corner of the throne room. The rest surrounded Yawen.

Only then did Baili release her control and sag with relief. Chouko slipped to her side, and Baili whispered thanks as she leaned on her friend. Yawen, battered and drenched, makeup streaked and half washed away, still struggled vainly as the guards bound her hands. Another group of guards dragged in Lanfen, who fought and kicked until she noticed Yawen's state.

Xiang helped Emperor Yijun to his throne, then stood beside him. Both looked equally grim and regal as the guards forced Yawen and Lanfen to kneel before them. The emperor gazed at the pair for a moment before he spoke. "Zhu Yawen, Empress of the Kingdom of Seven Rivers, once-wife of Emperor Zhu Aigui, you made a grievous choice today. Our nations have not been enemies for many years. Why attack now?"

Yawen didn't even try to look contrite. "You know of my land's situation. I seek what my land needs to survive."

"Small wonder that your nation dies, Yawen, when its empress would sacrifice her own daughter to gain aid which a treaty might have bought."

"We needed more than a treaty." Yawen glanced scornfully at Baili. "And had she not been born — of wish, not natural means — the prophecy would have been mine to fulfill."

"I have found that prophecies only succeed when fulfilled by the people for whom they are meant." The emperor paused. "This much you *have* done, Yawen: your land *shall* be made whole and our kingdoms united, but not in the way you planned. You dreamed of a world empire with yourself on the throne, but instead, you wrote the doom of yourself and your servants."

At this, Lanfen threw herself facedown on the floor. "Oh, imperial majesty, have mercy! I acted on the orders of my empress; I bear no ill will towards you or the princess!"

Baili barely suppressed a Chouko-like huff. "If you desired no harm, perhaps you should not have ordered the soldiers to kill me, or at least you might have warned me of what was ahead. You are clever, Lanfen. You could have found another option."

"Indeed." The emperor gave Lanfen a look of disdain. "You knew the reason for your orders and had the opportunity to choose otherwise, but you persisted and so you will be punished." The emperor turned back to Yawen. "In any other circumstance, I would not pass judgment on another ruler, yet your deeds and speech testify against you. You plot against your daughter, whom you should protect, and against a kingdom with which you promised peace. For this, you shall die, and your servant with you. Your kingdom shall be added to mine; my family shall rule your holdings and your country shall be our province. Your husband's son, when he comes of my age, may rule as my vassal, but until then, one of my own shall stand as regent for him. And in the throne which you intended for yourself, my son and your daughter shall one day sit. Do you understand, Yawen? All you desired shall go to others; all you inflicted on others instead falls upon you."

Yawen did not respond, only stared bitterly, her hands fists, her face pale with rage. Lanfen sobbed beside her, babbling that she wasn't to blame.

The emperor beckoned to his guards. "Take these and their soldiers to the cells, but treat them with courtesy as they await their fates." He turned to Baili and her companions, who had gathered around her. "As for you, Princess Zhu Baili, I formally welcome you to my home and family."

Baili bowed, holding onto Chouko for support. "I thank you, honored majesty, for your welcome and for carrying out justice on my behalf."

"Such is the duty of kings and emperors, Princess. One day, you will learn that well." He placed a hand on Xiang's arm. "And you owe your thanks to Xiang as much as I, for he first suspected the truth and sought you out."

"Forgive me, honored father, but she owes me no thanks." Xiang stepped off the dais, crossed to Baili, and bowed with a smile. "I would have searched the farthest reaches of the world to find her, yet I cannot take all the credit. Without the efforts of Ganbaatar and his companions, I should have looked that long and far indeed, but with no success."

"Indeed." The emperor surveyed Baili's friends. Gan and Azuma both bowed in the soldiers' fashion: quickly, leaving their sword hands free. Ailin bent deeply. Chouko, still supporting Baili, dipped just enough to be polite. The emperor continued: "Master Ganbaatar and his companions will be rewarded in due time. Until then, let them be our honored guests." He raised his voice so the servants and nobles crowding the doorways could hear. "And now, let the feast prepared for the empress be put to better purpose: welcoming my son's true bride and honoring the prophecy's fulfillment." He beckoned to a steward. "Find attendants for Princess Baili and her companions, and see that the princess has the comfort and luxury she is due. What has been stolen from her, we shall restore."

The steward bowed and moved off, calling orders to other servants. Xiang took Baili's hand and smiled at her. "You are safe now, Baili-*shán*. You are home."

Baili shyly returned the smile. "I know. Thank you, Xiang-*rón*." She turned to her companions. "And thank all of you as well."

Chouko huffed. "I promised to protect you, and I have kept my promise. Now keep yours, *kuīnzuko*, and remember us as we remember you. That will be thanks enough."

Gan snorted a laugh. "*Erveekei*! The *günja* has been a good influence on you; that was nearly touching."

Chouko glared at him. He ignored it and bowed to Baili. "We shall miss you, *günja*. To know you has been both honor and blessing." Turning to Xiang, he added, "You say that she is safe with you, *taijin*. See that she is and that you treat her well. She has become a sister to me, and men of the Plains belong to their sisters as well as their wives, so sisters may call on brothers when husbands fail them."

Xiang, to his credit, didn't take offense at being threatened by a horse-keeper but instead bowed back to Gan. "As long as I live, Master Ganbaatar, my princess shall be the delight of my eyes and the joy of my heart. None shall touch her if I can stop them."

"Good." Gan smiled fiercely. "Then, as my people say, I pray that the skies shine upon your union, that the wind be ever at your backs, that your tents stand sturdy above your head, and that you may live happily so long as you stand beneath the skies."

Xiang pulled Baili to himself, supporting her as Chouko had. She leaned into him, resting her head against his shoulder, as he spoke. "And may the Divine shower His blessings upon you for as long as you live, Master Ganbaatar. As for myself and my princess . . ." Xiang glanced down at Baili with a smile. "We are together now, and our kingdom is safe, and so long as that is true, we will indeed be happy forever after."

EPILOGUE

"Princess Baili, Prince Xiang, Nakuhara Chouko is here as requested."

Baili looked up from her page of notes, sketches, and doodles, a smile spreading across her face. "Thank you —" she paused to recall the servant's name — "Aiya. You may go." She stood. "Chouko-*koyū*, I am glad to see you. Thank you for coming."

Chouko dipped in a partial bow. "I did not know I was allowed to refuse, *kuinzuko*." She glanced towards Xiang and raised an eyebrow. "Am I interrupting?"

"Only a little." Xiang gathered up the papers spread across Baili's receiving room table, shuffling them into a neat stack. "Loath as I am to admit it, we are nearly finished for the day, and so I will leave the two of you to speak privately."

Baili put a hand on his shoulder. "You need not go, Xiang-rón, if you do not wish to."

Xiang stood and tucked the papers into the crook of his arm. "I never wish to leave you, my princess.

But I fear your friend will not be pleased if I stay, and my father is surely wondering what has become of me. I should have been in his study half an hour ago. I will go now and tell him of what we have discussed." He bent, took her hand, and kissed her knuckles. "Until later, Baili-*shán*. My heart shall ache until I see you again."

Chouko rolled her eyes. Baili smiled and kissed his cheek as he straightened. Even after several weeks, Xiang's affections still made her heart sing, and she reveled in the fact that she could return them openly. "As shall mine. I will see you at dinner."

Not to be outdone, Xiang brushed a kiss against her cheek before stepping away. "Until dinner, then." With a final bow, he departed.

Chouko watched him go, then turned to face Baili. "Do I dare ask what you and your prince are planning before you are even married? Or was it just silks and flowers for the wedding?"

"My wedding was planned long before I arrived, Chouko-*koyū*. Our plans are more serious — though I think I already told you something of them." Baili gestured at the many low chairs placed near hers. "Will you sit with me?"

"As you wish." Chouko chose a seat near Baili's, but not facing her. "You truly plan to free those your kingdoms captured and return them to their homes, then?"

"I intend to try." Baili sat as well, glancing once again at her page of notes. "It is a larger task than I thought. I had not realized how many people had been torn from their homelands, and Xiang has pointed out that many of the nobles of both kingdoms will not be pleased at the prospect of losing their servants. But he is helping me figure out what may be done."

"Good." Chouko paused. "I know why you have asked me here. And it is not because of your project."

"Oh?" Baili picked up paper and charcoal and began a new sketch in the bottom corner. "You are so sure?"

Chouko snorted. "Of course. I am still no fool, and I have seen what came of your conversations with the others this past week. You took Ailin as an attendant — your choice or hers?"

"Both." Baili added a careful line to the parchment. "I offered to return her to Seven Rivers and give her a comfortable life there, but she wished to remain with me. So I then asked her if she would be my attendant, and she agreed."

"Hmph." Chouko might have been pleased. "And did you offer the same to Jialin?"

"I did, but she refused, as I am sure you know. She wished to stay with her brother, and Renshu does not believe his fortunes lie within the palace walls. He wished for land and enough wealth to make something of himself, and so that is what I gave him. The imperial family has plenty of both to spare." Baili glanced wistfully out the window. "I will be sorry when he leaves, but I do not doubt he will do well for them both."

"He and Nianzu will." Chouko almost smirked. "Perhaps Nianzu will finally say what he has meant to say to Jialin since they met, now that he has something to offer her. He took land and wealth as well, after all."

101

"And specified that it was to be near to Renshu and Jialin, yes."

"He did not mention that part." Chouko sniffed. "And Ganbaatar and Azuma are first among your personal guardsmen, foreigners though they are. I am surprised that Gan, at least, took the position — or that you offered it."

"Both chose to be loyal to me when that loyalty offered more risk than gain. Xiang and I do not think they will turn on me now." Baili pensively rested her charcoal against the paper. "As for their being foreigners, I offered to return both to their homes, but they too refused. Azuma's home is long conquered, part of the Middle Kingdoms now, and he wishes to fight for a princess once more. And Gan's land may still be free, but you heard his speech as well as I did. He believes there is more honor to be had here than in his homeland, and I am glad of it. If I am to make the changes I promised, I may need to call on his skills."

Chouko raised an eyebrow. "Gan does not think it beneath his honor to guard his enemies?"

"Gan, I believe, thinks it great honor that his once-enemies trust him enough to ask, and greater honor to protect his friends. He says that he would rather have that than whatever battle-glory he might chance upon among his own people." Baili added a final line to her doodle: a goose honking defiantly at the notes on the page.

"Hmph." Chouko folded her arms. "That accounts for all but me, then. So what plan do have for me? Do you intend to offer me some position in your service as well? Or do you think land and wealth will please me as it did Renshu, Jialin, and Nianzu?"

"Chouko-*koyū*, do I not know you better than that?" Baili set down her charcoal again but did not look at Chouko. "Much as I would like you by my side, that is not my first offer. I would not keep you here against your will. You said once that you wish to go to the Endless Plains and find a place among the clans. If that is still your desire, I have spoken to Gan, and he believes it is possible so long as he is able to send one of his fellow Plainsmen to guide you there and see that you are accepted. Or, if you have changed your mind and wish to return to your own country, Xiang and I will see that you may travel safely there and that you have whatever resources you need to reunite with your family and start a new life. Whatever you wish, I will do whatever I can to carry it out."

Chouko blinked twice. Her eyebrows rose. She opened her mouth, shut it, opened again, and finally regained her composure. "That is your offer, then? You do not try to keep me close so I am at your beck and call? Or am I no longer such a friend that you desire me nearby?"

"You will always be my friend, Chouko-*koyū*. Always, so long as I draw breath." Baili took a deep breath, steeled herself, and looked into Chouko's face. "I would love little more than to have you near, to continue to learn from you, to have you at my back and be myself at yours. If you choose to go, I will miss you until the sun ceases to rise and the moon sets and does not return. And if you wished to stay, truly I would ask you to serve at my side. The emperor has advisors; so too does the empress, and she has companions as well — those who are more than

103

advisors; who are her closest confidantes aside from the emperor and who speak the truths to her that others cannot. These days, it is not a position always filled, but I can think of few who could fill it better than you. Your advice and friendship would be a great treasure to me, especially as I seek to right the wrongs done to your countrymen and others like them."

Baili paused, composing her next words. "Yet you have dwelt long in a land for which you bear no love, and which has wronged you time and time again. If I were to force you to remain, I would be no better than those who brought you here, and I would break the promises I made to you. I will not do that, no matter how much I might wish you here. So, as I said, if you wish to go to the Plains, or back to the Fire Islands, or with Nianzu and Renshu and Jialin, or anywhere else, I will help you. My reward for you, my friend, is freedom to decide where you will go and what you do next."

"You will let me go anywhere I wish. Be anything I wish," Chouko said slowly. "You give me the freedom to choose. That is what you said?"

"It is. Anywhere, anything, so long as it breaks no laws. And whatever I can provide to help you in your new life, I will give." Baili swallowed hard, blinked back tears, as she waited to hear Chouko's decision and tried not to think about how she would soon lose a dear friend.

Chouko remained silent and thoughtful for some time, her face a mask of some emotion Baili couldn't identify. At last, after what felt like an eternity, she spoke. "Whatever I choose? Very well. I choose to stay, at least for now."

Baili shook herself as if coming out of a dream. "You — what? You will stay?"

Chouko raised an eyebrow. "What, *kuīnzuko*, you do not want me after all?"

"Of course I do, but — why?" Baili asked, bewildered. "You said before . . ."

"So I did. But you and Ganbaatar and your prince are all heroic fools, and someone besides Azuma must remain to give you good advice." Chouko smirked and then grew serious. "The kingdom I wished to leave is not the same as the kingdom in which I choose to stay. In the kingdom I choose, there is a princess who has made promises and a prince who will listen when she stands for those promises. But they will need people who know what they do not if they wish to carry out what they intend. And in the kingdom, there are friends who I find I do not wish to leave just yet. Someday I will go to the Plains or back to the Isles or wherever I please, but not today. For now, I will be your advisor and your companion and see what comes when you keep the promises you made. You will be a fine empress when the time comes, Baili-*koyū*, and I wish to be at your side at that time."

Baili nearly laughed with relief, but she restrained herself. Instead, she bowed and reached out to place her hand on Chouko's arm. "And I will be glad to have you there, Chouko-*koyū*. Together, we shall see the world changed and all the wrongs of this empire set right. Wait and see."

GLOSSARY

Terms from the Middle Kingdoms:

Duānkou de Taìyáng: A city located near the spot where the Taìyáng River exits the mountains. Literally, "Port of the Sun."

Duānkou de Yueláng: A city located on the Yueláng River. Literally, "Port of the Moon."

-rón: Honorific used when a lady addresses a man of the same or similar rank as she.

Shénme Jiāng: Heaven, literally "What Will Be."

Shi Chunshi: Imperial city of the Kingdom of Seven Rivers. Literally, "City of Many Waters."

Shi Tienkon: A city in the western part of the Kingdom of Three Peaks. Literally, "City of Sky."

Shi Xīng Jí: Imperial city of the Kingdom of Three Peaks. Literally, "City of Stars."

-shán: Honorific used when a man addresses a lady of the same or similar rank as he.

-shūni: Honorific used when a lady of high noble rank is addressed by an inferior. Using this honorific with the lady's family name rather than her personal name indicates greater respect and submission.

Taìyáng River: A river that runs through both Middle Kingdoms. Literally, River of the Sun.

-xiá: Honorific used for females in the imperial family, regardless of the speaker's rank.

Yueláng River: A river that begins north of the Kingdom of Three Peaks and meets the Taìyáng at Shi Xīng Jí. Literally, River of the Moon.

~~~~~

Terms from the Fire Islands:

Anata ni shukufu: Blessings to you. Traditional Fire Islands greeting.

Atana kanasha shimatsu.: My thanks to you. (formal)

Arishoto.: Thank you. (informal)

Hantū: Hunter

-himei: Fire Islands honorific for a princess or high noblewoman.

Jaken-sha: Derogatory term used by the people of the Fire Islands for the people of both Middle Kingdoms. Literally, "thieves" or "takers."

Kasai Shotō: Fire Islands.

Kanagi shimatsu.: Be welcome.

Kasenotoshi: A city-state in the Fire Islands. Literally, "The City of Rivers."

-koyū: Fire Islands honorific for a dear friend or companion. Gender-neutral.

Kuīnzuko: Princess, high lady.

Matsunomi: Idiomatic insult for a morally fallen leader, especially one who turns on or betrays his or her own people. Literally, "pine nut."

Sorashima: One of the Fire Islands. Literally, "Sky Island."

Yofukashi: Wayward woman, harlot, prostitute.

Yujinaijin: Literally, "friend-not-friend." Used to refer to someone who is closer to you than an acquaintance or ally but who isn't close enough to be called a true friend.

~~~~~

Terms from the Endless Plains:

Erveekei: Butterfly

Günja: Plains term used to refer to the favorite daughter of a clan ruler; may also refer to a princess or high female noble.

Taijin: Plains term used to refer to the son or second of a clan ruler; also may refer to a prince or high male noble.

ACKNOWLEDGMENTS

Although *Blood in the Snow* is my book, it would be a lie to say that I'm the only one responsible for its existence and publication. I've had amazing help and support from wonderful people through every stage of the writing, editing, and publishing process. To that end, thanks to several people are in order.

First and foremost, I would like to give a big thank you to Anne Elisabeth Stengl and Kendra E. Ardnek. *Blood in the Snow* was written for the last of Anne Elisabeth's Rooglewood Press competitions, and it was thanks to the comments of Anne Elisabeth and the other contest judges that I first realized, *oh, I might have something really worth publishing here.* However, I doubt I would have acted on that thought if it hadn't been for Kendra E. Ardnek. Not only did Kendra organize the Magic Mirrors release, but she also encouraged me to join and gave me a fair bit of guidance as I prepared *Blood in the Snow* for publication.

On that note, I also have to thank my awesome beta readers: Alina Kanaski, Emmarayn Redding, JLiessa44, Meghan Largent, Shawn Little, and Wyn Owens. Their feedback played a major role in making *Blood in the Snow* what it is today, and their enthusiasm was immensely encouraging.

Quite a few people also helped during the writing and initial editing process, namely the Rooglewood Contest Facebook crew and the other members of my July '16 Camp NaNoWriMo cabin. Although writing is a solitary pursuit in many respects, I greatly appreciated the community and motivation I found in both these groups. Many thanks to everyone — I won't list names for fear of forgetting someone, but you're all awesome.

And, going back all the way to the initial inspiration phase: Blood in the Snow would literally not exist if not for my wonderful sister, Rachel. Two years ago, on the night before Camp NaNoWriMo began, she stayed up with me as I tried to sort vague Snow White retelling ideas into a slightly more solid plot so I could start writing the next day. Since then, she has continued to be my sounding board and troubleshooting helper for numerous ideas and issues. She is, without a doubt, the best sister a writer — or anyone else — could ask for.

In addition, I have received a great deal of support and encouragement from my parents through everything leading up to this moment. Somehow, they always understand when their daughter decides to do crazy things like writing novels in the busiest months of the year for fun. For their love, their understanding, their encouragement, their patience, and their willingness to listen to me ramble about stories they never actually got to read, I am and will be eternally grateful.

Another big thanks to my roommate, Alana, who probably listened to as many story-related rants as any of my family members did and who forgave me when editing time occasionally cut into our other plans.

Finally, I am eternally thankful to my God, the Great Author of my life's story. He has been faithful through every twist and turn up to this point, and I cannot wait to see what He has planned for this next chapter of my life.

ABOUT THE AUTHOR

Sarah Pennington has been writing stories since before she actually knew how to write, and she has no intention of stopping anytime soon. She is perpetually in the middle of writing at least one or two novels, most of which are in the fantasy and fairy tale retelling genres. Sarah's first published work, *Blood in the Snow*, received a perfect score and Special Unicorn status in Rooglewood Press's *Five Poisoned Apples* contest. When she isn't writing, she enjoys knitting, photography, and trying to conquer her massive to-be-read list.

Sarah can be found online at sarahpennington.com. She also blogs at Light and Shadows (tpssaralightshadows.wordpress.com) and Dreams and Dragons (dreams-dragons.blogspot.com).

OTHER MAGIC MIRRORS TITLES

This book was published as part of the Magic Mirrors, a collection of seven unique and exciting retellings of *Snow White*. Check out these other titles, each showing a side of the tale you've never seen before!

Red as Snow
Kendra E. Ardnek

Snow needs a husband in order to claim her throne,
but it's hard to compete with a younger, prettier
stepmother.

A Twisted Fairy Tale.

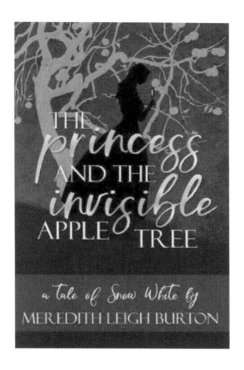

The Princess and the Invisible Apple Tree

Meredith Leigh Burton

Snowdrop didn't want a sister, but she and Rachel find their fates twisted together by a sinister enemy.

A Dark Reimagining

For Such a Time as This
Heather L.L. FitzGerald

It's a beauty pageant to determine the new queen –
but the deposed Vashti is not ready to relinquish her
power.
Fantasy Dystopia.

Overpowered
Kathryn McConaughy

Fleeing a terrible crime, Taliyah bat Shammai finds herself barred from the city of refuge. Can a band of seven landless fighters protect her from the Avenger of Blood?
Near Eastern Fantasy.

But One Life
Wyn Estelle Owens

Ginny serves the Revolution as a spy in New York City, but when her stepmother's Tory leanings endanger her life, will she be brave enough to do her duty?

Historical Fiction.

The Seven Drawers
Kendra E. Ardnek

After her father's death, Gwen's normal life takes a
turn for the crazy when a chest of drawers appears
in her bedroom.

Contemporary Fantasy